W9-CCM-388

ALSO BY PETER HANDKE

Don Juan

Don Juan

 HIS OWN VERSION

PETER HANDKE

TRANSLATED FROM THE GERMAN

BY KRISHNA WINSTON

FARRAR, STRAUS AND GIROUX

NEW YORK

Farrar, Straus and Giroux
18 West 18th Street, New York 10011

Copyright © 2004 by Suhrkamp Verlag Frankfurt am Main
Translation copyright © 2010 by Krishna Winston
All rights reserved
Distributed in Canada by D&M Publishers, Inc.
Printed in the United States of America
Originally published in German in 2004 by Suhrkamp Verlag, Germany
Published in the United States by Farrar, Straus and Giroux
First American edition, 2010

Library of Congress Cataloging-in-Publication Data
Handke, Peter.
    [Don Juan. English]
    Don Juan : his own version / Peter Handke ; translated from the
German by Krishna Winston.—1st American ed.
        p.   cm.
    ISBN 978-0-374-14231-5 (hardcover)
    1. Cooks—France—Fiction.   2. Don Juan (Legendary
character)—Fiction.   I. Winston, Krishna.   II. Title.

PT2668.A5D6613 2010
833'.914—dc22

                                            2009029526

Designed by Jonathan D. Lippincott

www.fsgbooks.com

1   3   5   7   9   10   8   6   4   2

Chi son' io tu non saprai.

(Who I am, you shall not discover.)

—Da Ponte/Mozart

Don Juan

Don Juan had always been looking for someone to listen to him. Then one fine day he found me. He told me his story, but in the third person rather than in the first. At least that is how I recall it now.

At the time in question, I was cooking only for myself, for the time being, in my country inn near the ruins of Port-Royal-des-Champs, which in the seventeenth century was France's most famous cloister, as well as its most infamous. There were a couple of guest rooms that I was using just then as part of my private quarters. I spent the entire winter and the early spring living in this fashion, preparing meals for myself and taking care of the house and grounds, but mainly reading, and now and then looking out one little old window or another in my inn, formerly a gatekeeper's lodge belonging to Port-Royal-in-the-Fields.

I had already lived for a long time without neighbors. And that was not my fault. I liked nothing better than having neighbors, and being a neighbor. But the concept of neighborliness had failed, or had it gone out of style? In my case, though, the failure could be attributed to the game of supply and demand. What I could supply, as an innkeeper and chef, was no longer demanded. I had failed as a businessman. Yet I still believe as much as ever in the ability of commerce to bring people together, believe in it as in little else; believe in the invigorating social game of selling and buying.

In May I pretty much gave up gardening in favor of simply watching how the vegetables I had planted or sown either thrived or withered. I used the same approach with the fruit trees I had planted a decade earlier, when I took over the gatekeeper's lodge and turned it into an inn. I made the rounds again and again, from morning to night, through the grounds, which were situated in the valley carved by a stream into the plateau of the Île-de-France. Holding a book in my hand, I checked on the apple, pear, and nut trees, but without otherwise lifting a finger. And during those weeks in early spring I continued steaming and stewing for myself, mostly out of habit. The neglected garden seemed to be recovering. Something new and fruitful was in the making.

Even my reading meant less and less to me. On the morning of that day when Don Juan turned up, on the run, I decided to give books a rest. Although I was in the middle of reading two seminal works, seminal not only for French literature and not only for the seventeenth century—Jean Racine's defense of the nuns of Port-Royal and Blaise Pascal's attack on the nuns' Jesuit detractors—I concluded from one minute to the next that I had read enough, at least for now. Read enough? My thought that morning was even more radical: "Enough of reading!" Yet I had been a reader all my life. A chef and a reader. What a chef. What a reader. I also realized why the crows had been cawing so ferociously of late: they were enraged at the state of the world. Or at mine?

Don Juan's coming on that May afternoon took the place of reading for me. It was more than a mere substitute. The very fact that it was "Don Juan," instead of all those devilishly clever Jesuit padres from the seventeenth century, and also instead of a Lucien Leuwen and Raskolnikov, let us say, or a Mynheer Peeperkorn, a Señor Buendía, an Inspector Maigret, came as a breath of fresh air. At the same time, Don Juan's arrival literally offered me the sense of a widening of my inner horizons, of bursting boundaries, that I usually experienced only from reading, from excited (and exciting), blissful reading. It could just as well have been Gawain, Lancelot, or Feirefiz, Parzival's piebald half brother—no, not him, after all! Or perhaps even Prince Myshkin. But it was Don Juan who came. And he was actually not altogether unlike those medieval heroes or vagabonds.

Did he come? Did he appear? It would be more accurate to say that he hurtled or somersaulted into my garden, over the wall, which was an extension of the inn's façade along the street. It was a truly beautiful day. After the kind of overcast morning so common in the Île-de-France, the sky had cleared, and now seemed to continue clearing, and clearing, and clearing. Yes, the afternoon stillness was deceiving, as always. But for the moment it predominated, and cast its spell. Long before Don Juan hove into sight, his panting could be heard. As a child in the country I had once witnessed a farm boy, or whatever he was, running from the constables. He raced past me on a path leading uphill, and at first nothing could be heard of his pursuers but their shouts of "Halt!" To this day I can see that boy's face, flushed and puffy, and his body, which looks shrunken, his pumping arms seeming all the longer. But what has stayed with me even more vividly is the sound he was making. It was both more than panting and less. It was also more than whistling and less that burst out of both of his lungs. Besides, it was really not a question of lungs. The sound I have in my ear breaks or explodes out of the entire person, and not from his insides but from his surface, his exterior, from every single patch of skin or pore. And it does not come from the boy alone but from several, a large number, a multitude, and that includes not just his pursuers, bellowing as they gain on him, but also nature's silent objects all around. This whirring and vibrating, no matter how unmistakably the hunted boy had reached the end of his strength, has stayed with me, representing an overwhelming power, an elemental force of sorts.

I had hardly heard Don Juan's breathing, far off on the horizon and at the same time very close, when I promptly had the runaway before me. The long-ago bellowing of the constables was replaced by the roar of a motorcycle.

As the rider gave gas, the engine's howl rose rhythmically, and it seemed to be coming ever closer to the garden,
bucking over everything in its path, unlike the breathing,
which had immediately filled the garden and continued to
fill it.

The ancient wall had crumbled a bit in one place, cre-
ating a sort of breach, which I had left that way on purpose.
That was where Don Juan came hurtling head over heels
onto my property. He had been preceded by a sort of spear,
or lance, that whizzed through the air in an arc and dug
itself into the earth right at my feet. The cat, which was
lying next to that spot in the grass, blinked a few times,
then went right back to sleep, and a sparrow—what other
bird could have pulled this off?— landed on the still quivering shaft, which then continued to quiver. In actuality the
lance was just a hazel branch, slightly pointed at the tip,
such as you could cut for yourself anywhere in the forests
around Port-Royal.

That boy fleeing years ago from the local constabulary
had not even noticed me. Unseeing, his pupils bleached
white in his fiery red face like those of a poached fish, he
had thudded past me, the child observing the scene (if it
was a powerful thudding, it was with his last reserves).
This Don Juan on the run did see me, however. As his body,
head and shoulders first, came flying through the breach,
not unlike the spear, he had me directly in his sights. And
even though this was the first time the two of us had laid
eyes on each other, this intruder immediately seemed
familiar. He had no need to introduce himself, which he

could not have managed anyway, his breathing nothing but a strange, uninterrupted singing. I knew I had Don Juan before me—and not just *some* Don Juan, but *the* Don Juan.

Not often, yet repeatedly, in my life, total strangers like this—they in particular—have seemed familiar at first sight, and in each case this sense of familiarity has proved consequential, without even needing to be deepened as we have come to know one another. This familiarity had potential. But whereas on the previous occasions (all too infrequent), the other person had become my confidant, when Don Juan turned up the opposite happened: his eyes sought me out first, and he immediately made it clear that the role of confidant for the story he had to unload was reserved for me.

Still, that farm boy on the run so long, long ago and the Don Juan before me had something in common. Both of them offered an image of festiveness. Indeed, that panting boy stumbling by had been dressed in his Sunday best, the standard outfit worn by country folk for going to church. And today's Don Juan was also festively dressed, though in an outfit that went with the blue May sky. Furthermore, his fleeing, like that fleeing long ago, itself exuded a festive air. Except that the glow that surrounded Don Juan came from inside him, whereas the boy's—well, where did it come from? No glow had emanated from him personally, none at all.

Had the motorcycle in hot pursuit got stuck in the Rhodon valley, still swampy in places even today? The roar of the engine kept coming from the same spot. No more revving. The vehicle hummed evenly, almost peaceably, at a distance. Don Juan and I positioned ourselves by the dip in the wall, and both of us peered out. Half hidden by the pale green riparian forest, a couple was sitting on the motorcycle, which at that very moment was turning and then chugged off, weaving in and out among the alders and birches. Apparently the enclosed grounds of the former monastery of Port-Royal-in-the-Fields still had the power to offer asylum. No one could be pursued inside its walls. Whoever entered was safe for the time being, no matter what terrible things he had done. Besides, the expression in the couple's eyes revealed that this Don Juan was not the one they had been chasing. The one they wanted to kill was different. The woman looked especially confused. The man even gave Don Juan a friendly wave as they rode off.

As would be expected of a contemporary and/or classic couple on a motorcycle, these two were all in leather, black leather, and wore helmets that resembled each other as only helmets can. Needless to say, the hair of the apparently young woman in back billowed out from under her helmet, and was some sort of blond. Riding along, the two of them, the man and the woman, looked rather like brother and sister, even twins. What counteracted that impression was the way the woman had her arms around the man from behind, and also the fact that under their leather outfits they were clearly stark naked. The two of them had pulled on their suits in a hurry, and all the buttons, snaps, and zippers were open, so that anything that could flap open was doing so. Leaves, blades of grass, bits of snail shells (along with remnants of snails), and pine needles clung to the half-bared back of the man, but only to his. The young woman's shoulder blades seemed a flawless white. At most we saw a plump poplar seed sticking to them for a moment—before it blew away. These were no brother and sister who had jumped on their bike and sped off, perhaps to confront Don Juan and destroy him. I puzzled over the pine needles on the man's back, pressed deep into his skin. For the entire Port-Royal region had only deciduous trees.

Don Juan's face, which was rather broad and flat, remained blotchy for a while, just as I had imagined Feirefiz's, Parzival's half brother, whose mother was a "Mooress," when I read Chrétien de Troyes. Except that Don Juan's blotches were not black and white like his predecessor's but red and white, dark red and white. Also, the pattern was confined to his face, not spread over his entire body like my Feirefiz's. Even his neck was free of blotches. So only the surface of the redskin's face was checkered like a chessboard. His eyes were large, and hardly clouded from running; nor were they altogether devoid of mirth. I should consider him as real as anything could be, he told me, and he snapped shut the switchblade in his hand. Then he indicated to me that he was hungry. Sweaty and dehydrated though he was, he did not ask for something to drink but rather for something to eat. And when I, the chef, promptly went in to fix something for him, I was making it plain that I understood him. And how real this person was! I no longer recall the language in which Don Juan addressed me on that May afternoon near the ruins of Port-Royal-in-the-Fields. Whatever: I understood him somehow or other.

I had pushed all my lawn furniture into a corner formed by the wall, and was intentionally letting it rot. So now I brought out a chair from the kitchen for my guest. He walked backward to reach it. On this, the first day of the week that Don Juan would spend with me, I initially assumed that his habit of going backward allowed him to keep his eye on any danger or threat—for instance, from the motorcycle couple. But I soon noticed that his expression was not vigilant in the slightest. He certainly looked awake, but not watchful. Nor did he dart glances in one direction and then in the other or over his shoulder; as he backed up, he gazed straight ahead in the direction from which he had come. For someone like Don Juan, I would have expected this direction to be either the west, with the castles of Normandy and those monasteries still in operation in and around Chartres, or, more likely, the east, with the former residence of the Sun King not that far away at Versailles, and most likely Paris, not much more distant. But he had come running and hurtling into the Rhodon valley from the fields to the north, where the new towns of the Île-de-France were located, blocks and blocks of apartment houses, the towns' centers occupied almost exclusively by office buildings, the closest of these new towns being Saint-Quentin-en-Yvelines. On the other hand, that direction made sense in conjunction with the leather-clad motorcycle couple. And wasn't there at least one fir tree between the Ville Nouvelle and the ruins of the old abbey here, one in particular: The lone cedar on the edge of a residual patch of woods? The most splendid and sturdy growing thing in that entire landscape?

While I cooked for Don Juan, I watched him through the open window of my ground-floor restaurant kitchen—the house had only that one floor, though it was spacious. As he sat out there in the May sunlight, he began to watch me bustling about. Now and then he would get up and place a few ingredients on the windowsill for me, items he dug out of the pockets of his dress coat. No need for him to explain that he had collected these delicacies along the way while he was on the run. Yet the sorrel, stalks of wild asparagus, the St. George's mushrooms, with their characteristic springtime scent of freshly ground flour, did not give the impression of having been snatched or dug out in blind haste. Don Juan was used to being on the run and had had plenty of practice. He was in his element, or in one of his elements. Not that being on the run meant he had no fear and anxiety. Rather, fear and anxiety made him see better, more clearly, more spatially. This more spatial seeing: Didn't it result from the fact that while running he repeatedly whirled around and sometimes also ran backward? And at the same time he had even managed to prepare his finds for cooking—pared, rinsed, and scrubbed them. So running away helped Don Juan gain time? And I was almost irked that he, the newcomer to this area, had found all these fairly well hidden delicacies just like that, these treasures for which I, the longtime resident and expert, had been peeling my eyes all spring, to no avail. A good while before April 23, the Feast of St. George, for whom these tastiest of all "little knights" were named, I had been stung by young nettles as I searched along the edges of all the forests in the western Île-de-France for even one of these round, pale harbingers and embodiments of the new year—impelled by a hope that, according to one of the books I was still reading, increasingly took on "an impudent quality." And here this interloper deposited an armful of these ardently desired mushroom caps on my kitchen counter, so long bereft. On the other hand, little knights: not a bad match for him and for the story to come.

Don Juan edged his chair closer and closer to my kitchen window. It inspired him, he said, to watch me cook. Inspired? In what way? He sat there as if collapsed into himself. That impression was reinforced by the tall grass, which I had not mowed for weeks—on purpose. With its tawny coat, the cat looked like a lion as it brushed through the grass. This cat belonged not to me but to one of the houses in Saint-Lambert-des-Bois, the only village near Port-Royal, a good kilometer or several spear tosses away (my property's only neighbors were the ruins of the monastery and the old pigeon tower); that afternoon the animal climbed over the wall on schedule and kept me company at a distance for a while, after which it resumed its rounds to god-knows-where. Not once, when it paid me its daily visit, had this cat greeted me properly, something I kept hoping for almost peevishly. In the cat's eyes, I did not exist. But it rubbed up against Don Juan and kept weaving between his legs, from in front, from behind, and so on. Swarms of butterflies, of different varieties and colors, also fluttered around the newcomer, a veritable battery of miniature flags, pennants, and standards; and more than a few of the butterflies even alighted on him, especially on his wrists, his eyebrows, his ears, sipping the beads of sweat that welled up constantly as he rested, all the more prolifically as a result of his flight; he served them as a drinking trough. And I saw the muskrat that lived under the rotting lawn furniture, the shyest creature I had ever met, sniffing at Don Juan's toes, its whiskers relaxed as if it had not a care in the world. And as I stepped outside, carrying the tray, an enormous crow was just flying over, holding something like a tennis ball in its beak, which it promptly dropped to the ground within Don Juan's reach, a passion fruit, probably snatched from a stall in the market—wasn't it market day in Rambouillet, not that far off? And at almost the same moment, a second crow, even blacker and more massive, which had been hiding unnoticed in the foliage of one of my trees, a horse chestnut whose leaves had unfurled during the previous week, came hurtling out—a bursting as if the trunk were exploding—and shot into the air after the first crow, while a hail of branches cascaded from the tree's crown, dead or broken branches, forming a nice pile of firewood in the grass.

Don Juan was asleep. He had propped his legs on the crumbling tabletop, which had previously served me as a reading stand. His legs were swollen. When he began to eat he had hardly managed to open his eyes, and then he kept them almost closed, after a brief flash of alertness. But his closed eyes now meant something else. In eating he had reinforced his capacity for perception. Or was it his imagination? No. And subsequently he fell into a rhythm that soon had nothing to do with whether he was enjoying the food. Or was his humming not so much rhythmic as melodic, a melody to which his whole body swayed, if almost imperceptibly? (Later in his story Don Juan forbade me to interrupt with questions and comments. Altogether, I should become more unquestioning, he remarked.)

He sat in the mild May sun as he talked, while I, his listener, took advantage of the partial shade provided by an elderberry bush that happened to be in bloom just then, its tiny—"teeny-tiny" was the current expression out here in the country—cream-colored blossoms, not even as big as shirt buttons, shooting periodically down into the special elderberry grass without even a wind gust to propel them. The sporadic hail of blossoms crossed paths with the winged poplar seeds roaming around constantly, all day long, all week long, not only through the grounds and ruins of Port-Royal but also through the branching system of valleys carved by watercourses in the western Île-de-France. These airy and translucent flocks of flying objects seemed to loosen and lighten everything heavy, massive, stony, anchored, earthbound. As they whizzed by they made such things weightless, or at least less weighty. It was the period between the feasts of the Ascension and Pentecost, and more often than usual church bells echoed through the riparian forests with their tangles of woody vines. After the first and before the second they sounded from Saint-Lambert, in whose churchyard a mass grave held the remains of the nuns of Port-Royal, ostracized as heretics. Police cars kept driving by on the road, a mere spur leading to the ruins. They drove slowly, without a sound, then turned and made their way back, searching for who-knows-whom. One day a tornado in the form of a bomber squadron burst over the grounds of the inn, nothing special in and of itself—because the plateaus above the seemingly safe little valleys are home to a number of military airfields, that of Villacoublay, and that of Saint-Cyr with the military academy—but unusual nonetheless because squadron after squadron, made up of all different types of planes, almost brushing the treetops, churned up the air and darkened the blue of the May sky as they took part in pan-European maneuvers or who-knows-what.

Don Juan had changed his clothes. Or perhaps he had merely reversed his cloak. At any rate, he looked ready for a journey. The impression was reinforced when he stood up now and then and took a few steps backward, as if he were checking to see whether a conveyance had arrived. He murmured his first story to himself, probably, I thought, because this experience, the incident with the leather-clad bikers, had just taken place. It was not ready for telling. Thus there was no material to embellish. For now all he could do was pin down the facts, muttering a few cues to himself. He saw himself as still too prominent in the story; only when it was no longer about him could he embellish at will. With the passage of time I have come to see the situation differently. He also wanted no music to go with his story, any kind of music. He claimed it made him incapable. Incapable of what? Incapable.

On that particular day he was walking along unsuspectingly under the May sky of the Île-de-France, an especially expansive sky. Even nowadays, although the network of roads is becoming increasingly dense, it was possible to cut across the fields, which offered a pleasure perhaps entirely different from that of earlier times. He had landed in this region only that morning—landed in the literal sense, in a plane. He had spent the previous night and day in a foreign country, as indeed he had been in a different part of the world every day, and not merely in our Europe.

The area around Port-Royal looks like a single plain, yet when you cross it, it turns out to have all kinds of crags and fissures, carved by the many brooks, with the Bièvre functioning as the collector of all the others as they flow toward the Seine basin: what was masquerading as a plain turns out to be a plateau with deep gullies and gorges. The settled parts, particularly the new housing developments that sprawl both horizontally and vertically and the office complexes and factories, are located almost exclusively up on the plateau, which is quite barren and very windy.

The few remaining stands of trees bear no resemblance to real forests. On the other hand, the valleys or canyons created by the brooks are all thickly wooded, with oaks and edible chestnuts on the slopes and alluvial alder and poplar forests at the bottom, interrupted by clearings once occupied by old mills, now either in ruins or transformed into tree farms or riding stables. The brooks' headwater areas remained relatively untouched through the centuries, without sizeable buildings, the notable exception being Port-Royal, at the head of the Rhodon gorge, half an hour's ride from Paris, which formed almost a whole town, or rather fort, a fortress of the spirit, of a particular spirit of adventure. (I am adding all this detail not only because I have become so fond of the district around the ruins of Port-Royal, but also because I picture it as the right setting, or a possible setting, or at least the obvious setting, for the story I have to tell now, for something of the moment, or for the moment altogether, as perhaps the desolate walls of the Italian industrial suburbs were for Antonioni's films, and the sculpted sandstone buttes of America's Monument Valley were for John Ford's Westerns.)

The sister valley of the Rhodon valley is that of the Mérantaise, right by Saint-Quentin. Its upper course, likewise carved into the plateau, is free of settlements; in some spots there is an almost impenetrable thicket of woody vines and blackberry canes. He had passed through there that same morning, my Don Juan. Initially he had still followed woodland trails. He knew how to make himself inconspicuous. The joggers and riders, of whom there were quite a few, never noticed him. If anyone would have looked good on a horse, it was he—but perhaps not, after all. He jumped into the bushes, out of habit and a spirit of adventure. His goal was to be in control of his time; he described that as his chief occupation, or at least what gave it pizzazz. So he set his course for the cedar that stood out even at a distance, rising above a clearing in the meadows along the Mérantaise, a dark, spreading form beyond the shimmering tangle of primeval forest—even though this diverted him from his original route.

Just as a solitary mushroom-gatherer sometimes comes upon a dead body, or so they say, Don Juan suddenly came upon the naked couple as he was cutting through the forest. He promptly stopped in his tracks. The woman was most visible through the underbrush, a rear view. All the terms, whether euphemistic or coarse, for what the couple were doing or what was happening with them had seemed inadequate approximations up to then, and will remain so. Of the man, Don Juan could see almost nothing except a bent knee. Nor could he hear any sound from the couple. They were lying in a sort of hollow, and he was standing at least "a stone's throw away," and the rushing of the brook and the rustling of the leaves were loud.

Don Juan's first impulse: to beat a silent retreat. But then he decided to stay and watch. It was a conscious, sober decision. He had to take in those two, whose bodies were conjoined and remained joined. There could be no question of averting his eyes. It was his duty now to register and to measure. To measure what? Don Juan did not know.

At all events, he watched without emotion and also without a breath of excitement. All he felt was astonishment, calm, natural astonishment. And in time that became a sort of frisson, though entirely different from the kind one experienced upon overhearing the goings-on in the hotel room next door, which as a rule was more of a bristling, with every hair standing on end.

It was obvious that the two of them had no sense that what they were doing there was secret, was anything they had to hide. They were performing not merely for chance onlookers but for the whole world. They were putting on a show. The act could not possibly be carried out more proudly or monumentally. The blond or bleached woman in particular visibly transformed this remote semi-wilderness, with flowering broom all around and the cedar nearby, into a stage, which for these very long moments really did represent the world. She played with the sun—now on her shoulders, now on her hips, now more and more on her buttocks—weaving like a dancer, a snake charmer. How proud she looked as she worked away, her back arched high. And it seemed as if only she were working (and as if her work was what mattered, and as if this were the best thing, if not the only thing, she had to offer the world, or whomever); the man beneath her was a mere prompter, so to speak, at her service, her tool, and thus almost invisible. With the man invisible and the woman radiating far and wide, this sight could also have been a stock scene from a film, yet its nature was fundamentally different, and not merely because Don Juan was observing it from a considerable distance, rather than from close up as in a film; even viewed this way, the scene loomed large, but that certainly had nothing to do with a close-up.

Not until the week following this experience, when Don Juan was thinking about the couple, celebrating their one-week anniversary, as it were—he was sure he was celebrating it, and how!—did it occur to him that the labiate flowers on the broom branches framing the couple had been intensely yellow. And that the wind had whipped those intensely yellow branches apart and together. From the cedar came the whooshing characteristic of cedar limbs. High above, almost unbelievably high for a bird, circled one of those eagles that normally waited for those particularly clear, still days that came only at the height of summer to leave their nesting places or refuges in the Rambouillet forest for an excursion to the skies closer to Paris. A few wasps could be heard rubbing on a weathered woodpile, just as they were doing on one of the wooden tables here in my garden while Don Juan described the scene; May was their nest-building month. From a branch above the Mérantaise brook dangled or swayed something longish and striped, much lighter than a shoe, for instance, or a piece of tape from an audiocassette; only a shed snakeskin could be that weightless. So snakes still lived in the Port-Royal region—or had returned. A cone from the previous year dropped from the cedar and rolled toward the couple. Mica sand glittered in the fishless rill, and the sound of tractors came from the fields up on the plateau. Along the edge of the forest on the opposite slope a family group, including grandparents, parents, and children, was laying out a picnic, and on one of the numerous rural roads a school bus was passing, the children all piled into the back, and the air was full of those little brown moths that always look like three whenever two of them are fluttering around each other.

Nonetheless, Don Juan felt disappointed by the couple in the end. The whole thing turned all too predictable. The two of them became audible. The woman's cries could be heard, and from the man came a kind of muttering, grunting, and growling. She tipped forward, and he ran one hand over her back while with the other he scratched his knee, which was bent again. After crying out she uttered something along the lines of "love," and he murmured something similar. Don Juan should have left the scene sooner. At this point it was no help that a cuckoo piped up, calling not in a dyad but in a triad, as if stuttering. Don Juan continued to watch conscientiously, but he was counting the seconds as he did so, or rather merely counting, as one does when forced to be somewhere against one's will or when time is hanging heavy. And for Don Juan time was a problem, the problem.

Not until the two naked people in the hollow were apparently attacked by flies and ants did he turn to leave. Actually the insects had been there all along, but only now did they seem to start annoying the couple. Up to the last moment Don Juan had been waiting for something to happen with the two of them that would alter the course of events. What, for instance? No questions! he scolded me.

As he turned to leave, he stepped on a fallen branch, and the couple became aware of him. He corrected himself: rather than the sound of cracking wood it was his sighing, the listener's sighing, that startled the two of them. Sighing in disappointment? No more questions now! At any rate, I have hardly ever heard a sigh like Don Juan's. And all week long, both when he was telling his story and when he was simply sitting there in silence, he sighed repeatedly. It was the sigh of an old man, and at the same time that of a child. It was exceedingly soft, even gentle, yet audible through any noise—the intermittent roar of the superhighway that periodically filled the Rhodon valley these days, or the drone of the bombers, the rhythm of whose Pentecost maneuvers resounded overhead all week long. Don Juan's sigh filled me with confidence, and not only in that one person.

To the lovers, however, that sigh signaled betrayal. What enraged them was not that someone had been watching them. The reason they pulled on their gear and came hurtling toward him on their bike was that with his sigh the spectator had demeaned the experience they had just shared, an experience that was perhaps still quivering between them. And as always, though always in different circumstances, Don Juan did not want to flee. He thought he should not flee. He must not flee. And as always there was no choice: he had to flee.

In this landscape he had the advantage: because he was on foot, he could cut straight across brooks and through underbrush, while the two on the motorcycle had to go the long way around, finding the dirt roads between fields and looking for the infrequent bridges. Now and then he even took his time. Part of it was that he occasionally walked backward, an old habit and not meant as a taunt. Yet it obviously irritated his pursuers, for eventually they boldly took off after him, over rough terrain and smooth, ignoring all obstacles. Now they were right behind him, and at last he had to take to his heels. They were shouting at him. Actually they were merely calling out to him, the tone almost friendly. Maybe he should have simply stopped running and faced them. Except that he would have had nothing to say to them. Not until a week later, still in my garden, could he turn to the now distant couple and wish them good luck and a life full of surprises.

To tell his actual story, on the evening of the day he arrived in Port-Royal-des-Champs, Don Juan started with the day that fell exactly a week earlier, when he was still in Tbilisi, in Georgia. He did not serve up the story of his life, or even that of the past year, only the most recent seven days, working his way through that week, day by day, on the days that followed. On this Monday, for example, the previous Monday came to mind, more vividly, yet also more matter-of-factly and calmly, than would ever have been the case with the previous Tuesday, or, let us say, the Monday of a month earlier, and that pattern held as he cast his thoughts back. "On Monday, exactly a week ago"—and already the images came rushing in, the images of the entire day, unbidden. These images from that day precisely a week earlier came to life, presented themselves as they had not presented themselves at the time, took their places, lined up quietly, without the hoopla of self-conscious remembering, without making a show of reaching into the past, without affecting a resonant voice. If it had a rhythm, then it was that of an orderly progression free of hasty interruptions, with matters small and large weighted equally, nothing large anymore, but also nothing small.

That was the form it took. That was how I heard Don Juan recounting his week, his style of narration probably determined to some extent by his having been in a different place every day, by his having been on the move all week long. Don Juan was not settled. A settled Don Juan would have had nothing to tell about those seven days, or at least not in this fashion, even if he had had similar experiences. A week narrated in this way, rather than the tale of a single day or a year, seemed right for someone like this Don Juan. But it was also right for me. And it was right for various others as well, if not in wartime then in a precarious and threatened time of peace.

In finding words for the seven stations of his week, Don Juan imbued them with reality and turned them to practical effect. And his story became a narrative without any piquant details. Not that he avoided such details; they were simply out of the picture for him from the beginning. It was obvious that they were not to be mentioned. "Piquant details" were not to be narrated. Indeed, they did not exist. And from the outset I would not have wanted to hear them. As I saw it, only in their absence did Don

Juan's adventures acquire a significance above and beyond his person—and ultimately they did strike me as
adventures. Certainly details did turn up as he cast his
memory back to the previous week, more and more of
them, but of a different sort, and adventurous in an unusual sense.

During those seven days when Don Juan sat in my
garden and told his story, to me and at the same time to
himself, he did not once ask who I was, where I came
from, how things stood with me. That did me good. My
only regular visitor in the previous months had been the
curé of Saint-Lambert-des-Bois, who made my situation
more untenable by implying that he was the only person
I had left, the very last; often I did not realize how alone I
was until the priest turned up, and after he left, my solitude gnawed at me, and gnawed and gnawed, and I pictured myself as one of the people whom the man in black
stopped in to see on their deathbeds as he made his sporadic rounds through that region; these visits had become
his main occupation. "Ah, my dying parishioners!" he
blurted out one time.

I cooked, and Don Juan told his story. After a while we
began to eat together at the table in the garden. How my
kitchen came to life! There is nothing more heartwarm-
ing, at least to my mind, than a kitchen in which someone
is bustling about, preparing all the dishes with gusto. Often
I involuntarily balanced on one leg, as in the old days, or
actually leaped like a mountain goat from one corner to
the other. And I ritualistically dried my hands on my

shirt, hanging loose over my pants, as I had once done on my chef's apron. During his weeklong stay, my guest never lifted a finger. He was used to being served hand and foot. True, I did not ask where his servant was. He would turn up in the story when the moment was right; and in fact that was exactly what happened. Don Juan seemed not to lift a finger—yet every time I came into the kitchen in the morning I would find some new ingredient, and it was not only flavorings and garnishes: a little sack of peppercorns from Szechuan, a coal black spring truffle from Turkey, a log of sheep's cheese from La Mancha, a fistful of wild rice from Brazil—as if gathered by him—a bowl of hummus from Damascus. Yet he had arrived without any luggage. All week long I did not have to go to the supermarket, of which I was thoroughly sick by now.

Not that we spent all that time in the house or the garden. Don Juan did not launch into his storytelling until evening, after supper, our only proper meal, and Port-Royal lay so far to the west that on those May days it stayed light almost to the end of the evening news, which we watched on television. During the day we roamed through the area's wooded river valleys and newly settled plateau. One time we set out in a straight line to the palace of Rambouillet, where suddenly, who knows why, dogs were unleashed on us, though they were interested only in Don Juan. On another day we headed east, in the opposite direction, to the plateau of Saclay, where we found the nuclear power plant surrounded by police cars, fire engines, and ambulances, as sirens blared unceasingly over the plateau. At the same time we watched two lizards copulating motionlessly in a hole in the ground near our feet, while in the air two flies circled, hooked together. On a third day we went north to the legendary springs that formed the source of the Bièvre, which we did not find because we lost our way in the labyrinth recently laid out in honor of the springs (the main spring, as we heard later from someone who had had better luck finding it, had been transformed into a fountain). On the fourth day we took the local bus to the "Jean Renoir" movie house in Trappes, where we saw a film in which a woman wanted to seduce a man into dying with her—into becoming totally wrapped up in her, which grew more and more irresistible to him from scene to scene and eventually inescapable, signifying the end for the man, as well as the woman. On the fifth day we merely took the short path uphill from the Rhodon to the road leading to Saint-Rémy-lès-Chevreuse, and from the bus stop there watched the local buses, most of which drove right past us without stopping. On the next-to-last day of the week, however, we stayed in my inn, which we furthermore had to lock up tight and partially barricade, for it had come under siege from women trying to get at Don Juan. During the last two storytelling evenings a threat hung over us, an increasingly dicey situation.

Don Juan was orphaned, and not in any figurative sense. Years earlier he had lost the person closest to him, not his father or his mother, but his child, his only child, or at least so it seemed to me. So one could also become an orphan when one's child died, and how. Or maybe his woman had died, the only one he loved?

He had set out for Georgia in his usual way, without any destination in particular. What drove him was nothing but his inconsolability and his sorrow. To transport his sorrow through the world and transmit it to the world. Don Juan lived off his sorrow as a source of strength. It was bigger than he was and transcended him. Armored in it, so to speak, and not merely so to speak, he knew that although he was not immortal he was invulnerable. Sorrow was something that made him impetuous, and, in an opposite and equal reaction (or rather action by action), completely permeable and open to whatever might happen, while at the same time invisible when necessary. His sorrow furnished provisions for his journey. It nourished him in every respect. As a result he had no major needs. Such needs did not even rear their heads. Yet he kept having to ward off the idea that sorrow made the ideal earthly life possible, applicable also to others (see "transmit sorrow to the world"). His sorrowing, fundamental rather than episodic, was an activity.

For years now Don Juan had had no regular human intercourse. At most there were chance encounters during his travels, out of mind as soon as the shared paths diverged. In the nature of things, not a few of these encounters involved women, and not bad-looking women, either (although with the passing years the number of real beauties to be met on the road was becoming ever smaller, at least in public places such as streets, city squares, and on journeys—as if they preferred to stay home, sequestered in the most remote nooks, or if they traveled at all, they did so in the depths of night and by undisclosed paths). Yet these women, attracted to Don Juan if he so much as allowed them to catch sight of him, attracted especially by his aura of profound sorrow, which in their eyes was a form of strength, always turned their backs on him after taking the first small step, speaking the first word. Whatever the case, he did not respond, was deaf and blind to them, at least as individual and female beings. Indeed he avoided speaking, even guarded against opening his mouth for anything resembling a conversation, as if departing from wordlessness would result in a loss of strength and betrayal of his peripatetic ways. How differently Don Juan had behaved before being orphaned, during the first half of his life.

Upon landing in Tbilisi he found that a destination offered itself after all. As almost always happened, this destination turned up by chance, simultaneously with his arriving in some place that at first seemed random. He would set out for the Caucasian piedmont he had just flown over, which spread across the entire region, and he would go directly from the airport. He would then turn around and head for the city of Tbilisi in the evening, or whenever he felt like it; he was the master of his time. At first the city would look like every other city he had seen in the past—that was the pattern by now—yet he knew that later on the specific features unique to Tbilisi would reveal themselves: the foreign and characteristic qualities of today's cities were no longer obvious; they had to be ferreted out, and that was an essential component of Don Juan's adventures. The idea—and it was an idea—came to him when he caught sight of the Georgian script— smaller script under the large Roman lettering in the arrival terminal (no longer a barrack-like building, and also no longer with passengers carrying chickens and rabbits in cages): in its density, rhythmic qualities, and roundness this writing mirrored the contours of the Caucasian foothills. No help for it: he had to head in that direction, in a new burst of sorrow-energy that revitalized his surroundings as well.

In the time before his loss Don Juan actually had taken it for granted that he would be waited on. Every new acquaintance soon came to see himself as part of Don Juan's worldwide cohort of servants. Without a moment's hesitation Don Juan would send him to get a book, medicine, some object left behind at a previous way station. No explicit order was required; a mere remark was enough: "I forgot my hat in . . ." (On the other hand, Don Juan also never asked for anything: his observation simply had to be followed up on.) In the twinkling of an eye he could become the other person's servant, whether that person was someone he knew or a stranger. And how he could serve, or rather, be of service! Each time it was a wordless and unbidden fetching, hopping to it, and giving a leg up, unobtrusive and without any servile bowing and scraping, and once done, as if in passing, it immediately became anonymous, as he himself took on an anonymous quality as a helper. And his temporary identity as a servant or aide was always noted by the servants without surprise. Or rather, it went almost unnoticed, and likewise elicited no expressions of gratitude, no remuneration. Yet his effect on those he assisted in this way was more than that of a silent servant, incomparably more.

For his journey to the plains at the foot of the Caucasus Don Juan took on a servant, for the first time in a long while. At least he immediately treated the driver as such, and the driver not only put up with it but seemed to have been waiting for it. He was standing on the edge of the airfield beside his old Russian car, and was holding the car or coach door open for Don Juan, and for him alone, while he was still a good way off. The two of them promptly came to an agreement, without anything being said. And this agreement extends beyond one day's service to an unspecified stretch of time, for who knows how long. The man seemed more like a longtime trusted partner than a newly hired servant; again it was that strange phenomenon of trust that so often sprang up between Don Juan and strangers, though in an entirely different way with women. This partner and traveling companion had already laid in enough provisions and fuel for a good week. If Don Juan spoke to him at all, it was in the customary pleasantries. And the new servant was dressed far more elegantly than his boss, in a dark, double-breasted suit, with a blindingly white pocket square, on either side of which small bunches of multicolored May blossoms peeped out. The whole car was scented with them, or with the driver's strangely delicate perfume. Apparently he had decked himself out this way for a particular festive occasion.

For the first time since the loss of his child, Don Juan felt jolted out of the equanimity that his inconsolable sorrow and his avoidance of all involvements had afforded him. The moment he awakened from his brief in-flight dream, his uneasiness had returned, an uneasiness with which he was familiar, all too familiar. This uneasiness manifested itself as follows: from one minute to the next he was no longer the master of his own time. Or: time was no longer his element. Or: the moments turned into seconds. For instance, instead of watching, listening, breathing, and so forth, Don Juan started to count. And he counted not just the seconds but everything, mechanically or automatically, everything that came within range of his automatic counting mechanism—he now consisted of nothing else: the rows of seats in the plane, the eyelets in his shoes, the little hairs in the eyebrows of the person seated next to him. Not that he suddenly felt bored; it was more serious than that: Don Juan had fallen out of the game of time, that unobtrusive, amiable game. But maybe that was the most serious form of boredom. In the past, this counting could be relied on to stop if he focused intently on another person, at least for a certain length of time, if he purposefully sought another's company. As now happened once he became a passenger in that automobile crammed with stuff.

After Russia, still shivering in the last chill of winter—the remaining snow piles in the rearmost of the rear courtyards a dingy gray, indistinguishable from sand—the soft air of the southern Caucasus felt warm, the embodiment of warmth. The sun was shining. As they drove, the two men had the sun at their backs more and more, and the landscape up ahead, rising gently toward the mountains, appeared in a relief of a clarity usually seen only in models, made, for instance, of papier maché. Yet there was nothing papery, nothing hollow here: everything looked compacted, weighty, intermingled, as if inextricably; clay with marl with rock outcroppings with taproots with basket roots, sulfur yellow with brick red with salt gray with coal black. The sandy stretches, too, neither soft nor loose but packed as firmly as mortar and baked hard; anyone who went to pick up a handful would end up with bloody nails, and not a grain of the presumptive sand clinging to his fingertips. Likewise there was not a cloud of dust to be seen, even though for long stretches the ground had hardly any vegetation (the apparent sandscape lying there as naked as white dunes), and even though a wind gust as sudden as it was powerful repeatedly swept through, coming each time from a different direction. The piedmont or balcony presented itself as seductive, uniting all the senses, only to be revealed as literally repellent and inaccessible. It beckoned as if magnetically toward its interior, but then turned out to have no interior. Upon arriving in this region a week earlier, Don Juan was reminded of the Badlands in South Dakota, where a system of broad, deep fissures in a vast expanse of sedimentary formations— each fissure distinct from the others—suggested a valley stretching for many miles yet without exception led no-where, or merely to naked, scarred walls of clay, or to the ends of washed-out gorges that had been bone-dry for millennia. But now, a week later, as he described it to me, he had the opposite feeling about this region at the foot of the Caucasus: now those famous, even world-famous, Badlands receded into the distance, a mere prelude to and preliminary sketch of this almost nameless, seldom vis-ited terrain, or only a pale imitation of it. This terrain seemed infinitely more impressive than the Badlands, ini tially so exemplary. It was unquestionably there, in one re-spect or another, while the eminently filmable Badlands on the other hand . . . But the reason for Don Juan's de-scribing this landscape so exhaustively in his story was that all six of the following days' landscapes resembled this one in some way. Each new day saw him enter a new, often distant country, and every time the landscape in which the day's events unfolded was, or became, largely the same. For each subsequent station of the story he could thus dispense with sketching in the scene of the action (or lack thereof).

That morning the southern slopes of the Caucasus were by no means deserted. In retrospect the roadsides were veritably packed with people. As he conjured up an image for me, they were all on foot, and the only vehicle on the roads was the one driven by his servant. The Orient? Hardly a trace of that: in clothing and behavior and even smells, the East by now seemed completely part of the West, as the West seemed part of the East, and so forth. Perhaps the only specific element during those seven days was the constantly wafting May air and the poplar-seed fluff flitting above, below, and through it.

Among all those people moving along the roadside there was hardly even one whom Don Juan recognized as a solitary wanderer. He encountered only groups, always small ones, but innumerable. Had he not stopped counting the moment he stepped into the car, at the latest he would have stopped when he came upon these various processions or migratory peoples.

The driver was on his way to a wedding, and Don Juan, without having been invited, would of course attend as a guest. In the past he had often taken part in strangers' celebrations—only strangers'. To be sure, until this day in the Caucasus they had all been funerals. Only at burials could one simply join a group, no questions asked. At christenings, for instance, one corner of the church was usually set aside for the private event, or the whole church was reserved. But there was also something to be said for standing outside and catching an impression at a distance of the baby's damp hair or bald head, or seeing a cluster of First Communicants lingering in the sun after the ceremony, licking their ice cream cones.

On the last leg of the journey, before they got to the village where the wedding was taking place, Don Juan changed roles from passenger to driver; his servant, after giving his master directions, stretched out between the canisters and hampers on the backseat and instantly fell asleep. If being alone usually made one more receptive to one's surroundings, or at least to the significant details, that effect was magnified in the presence of someone who was asleep, especially when his sleep was as relaxed and deep as this new acquaintance's with his scratched face. (I noticed how often in his story Don Juan used the indefinite pronoun "one" instead of "I," as if it were self-evident that what he experienced was applicable to everyone; I wish I could have said the same of the ups and downs in my own life—actually more downs of late.)

In previous years he had not avoided the sight and sound of other people. Yet he had focused primarily on either very old or very young people, on children. He ignored the great mass in between, the seemingly more and more predominant majority. It did not exist and it did not matter. Don Juan was all the more fervently on the lookout every day for someone feeble and/or in need of protection. Noticing such a person and considering that person worthy of observation meant more and something different to him than immersing himself in nature of whatever kind. And conversely, being considered worthy of observation almost without fail gave these grizzled folks and twerps something like an injection of new life. Strangely, the oldsters, once they were taken in and appreciated, radiated this new life and seemed childlike, while the little and littlest ones suddenly seemed not old, exactly, but settled and positively worldly-wise—the smaller they were, the more settled and worldly-wise. Only one or two "categories" of human beings still had a face for Don Juan, and that seemed to be an increasingly small minority.

It was not due exclusively to the man asleep on the backseat that this state of affairs perhaps began to change a bit. And likewise it was not primarily the corpse lying there in its blood, with its eyes open, as they rounded a bend. (Or possibly it was, after all.) Whatever the case: during this drive Don Juan gradually encountered faces, faces of all ages, including those in midlife, which until recently had seemed particularly insignificant and formless. It was less their faces than their eyes. It was less forms than colors that gave faces to the people striding or dragging themselves along the roadside. That, too, a sign of a new age: that these eye colors, deep in the Caucasus, were not uniformly brown or black. Just as frequently a green would come along, a blue, a light or dark gray. And this was noteworthy: even when the faces were contorted with exhaustion, with hopelessness, with rage or hate, and here and there even with bloodlust, even when these eyes had an evil cast, or an absent one, or an arrogant one—the colors themselves, so long as one zeroed in on them and caused them to shine forth or dance in the light, were good, forming a range of eye colors. In their succession, precisely because without exception each pair of eyes was gazing in a different direction and as if into the void, these colors now created a pulse; pulsed toward someone or something. Just as one often felt tempted to stroke a child's head in passing (and now and then actually did so), and as one felt tempted to put one's arm around some elderly person on the street (which one had never actually done), one felt tempted to run one's fingertips over all, yes all, those eyes and eyeballs and brush them with one's lips; the colors were practically waiting for some such thing. ("One.") Although Don Juan was driving past them, a week later his movement seemed in retrospect like walking, very slow walking.

He was not the one who then initiated the exchange of glances with the bride. She fixed her eyes on him first. This happened in a hall, but seven days later he saw the young woman not under a roof but under the clear blue sky. The wedding party was eating at a long table, and the guests who, like him, had turned up unannounced, of whom there were not a few, had been seated without any fuss at a number of small tables. Don Juan was shown to the smallest table, in the most distant corner of the hall, without its feeling like a slight. Rather it was a combination of hospitality and considerateness, part of which was that he had the table to himself and at the same time could survey the entire hall, together with the village landscape outside the windows. His servant was apparently a member of the extended family and had a seat at the head table, from where he repeatedly came over to Don Juan's table and relieved the waiters of the necessity of serving his master.

Don Juan told me how startled he was to find the bride looking at him. It was not a come-on, just a widening of the eyes. Such beautiful eyes, and without any effort she made the most beautiful eyes at him with those beautiful eyes. And Don Juan's startled response was by no means alarmed. It was a sudden yet quiet awakening after a sleep lasting many years, or, more precisely, being in a daze. Quiet: because the constant murmur of his interior monologue suddenly ceased. His forehead seemed to open up. Yet at first he still felt racked by confusion. His mind once made up, he rose from his seat and then strode—toward her?—out of the hall.

The decision had been made at once, however. There was no going back. For Don Juan avoidance was out of the question; he had to take on this unknown woman; it was his duty. (Even though he did not constantly use the term "duty" in the presence of me, his listener, it was often implied.) By the evening of this day at the latest, an epoch in his life would come to an end, and indeed he now saw it as an epoch. The Caucasian village was located on a fairly bare rocky formation. As he traversed it in increasingly large arcs and then struck out into the surrounding pastures and fallow fields, taking one detour after another, he felt certain this was the last time for an indefinite period that he would register all the allegedly small or insignificant things that for an entire epoch had meant the world to him, more than any thing or any person. As in an earlier time, in a past long since inoperative, the phenomenon of woman would crowd out the thousands of little things, mundane but all the more lovable, would leave them no breathing space. Woman as a curse? As the curse of aridity?

At that point Don Juan did not yet know that this time he was wrong, at least in this respect, was wrong primarily about himself. So now, as he was tracing his arcs, he was saying farewell. The snow-covered expanses in the mountains to the north for the coming period or perhaps from now on would hold no reality for him. The hissing of the wind in the brambles: play that for me one more time, you bushes. The funeral procession, hardly more than a couple of older folks and a child following a casket up ahead, while behind him the wedding music changed, from the folk songs with which it had begun to more transcontinental tunes: just a brief lingering with you mourners. Farewell, clay yellow and marl red. Take care, labiate broom blossoms and ant trails. Goodbye forever, tufts of wool caught on the pasture fences.

Conjuring up that epoch no longer worked. The new era, the womantime, had him in its thrall; its force or effect had set in at the very moment Don Juan got up from his table in the corner and headed outdoors. And soon he was more than merely reconciled to the new era. To be sure, it signified danger! But that lit a fire under him again, at long last.

On his way back to the village, dogs cleared out of his way. A village cat, which could equally well be a wildcat, was rolling on its back under some bushes, and then kept brushing between his legs. Large black flying beetles attacked him, their buzzing swelling to a dull roar, or at least they were pretending to dive-bomb him. To Don Juan animals had always seemed like messengers—whose message he could not know and also did not want to know. And he treated them with special courtesy, addressing the pigs, the donkeys, and the ducks in the dried-up village pond as politely as people of substance, speaking to them in complete sentences, carefully chosen, old-fashioned, yet contemporary sentences. Whenever things got serious he began to speak in this manner, and that included his silent conversations with himself.

How lovely and good this long period of solitary roaming had been, without friendships, without enmities. He had harmed no one, had promised nothing to anyone, had had no obligations to anyone. And now he was on duty. And soon he would hurt, perhaps destroy, someone. Don Juan was fully aware, as he bowed toward the woman, that he had to expect to make an enemy (and he did not mean the bridegroom or the bride's father or brother), and in anticipation he even saw himself, or part of himself, as a kind of enemy, as the coldest, most evil sort of enemy. What to do? In removing himself from the fray, he would become a swindler and a traitor. In going to her, sooner or later he would inevitably turn her into the woman he had abandoned, the woman bent on revenge, though perhaps only in thought, which was often even more powerful from a distance. How lovely and good his solitude had been, and how sinister and tasteless, yes, ridiculous. Whatever would be would be. This much was certain: to evade the woman who wanted him now would be a particular kind of abandonment—a particularly cowardly and shameful form of desertion.

At the threshold to the wedding hall, Don Juan used a leaf from the lone tree in the courtyard to wipe the dirt off his shoes. He rubbed his hands with a bunch of wild thyme. He opened and closed his eye several times fast, meanwhile slapping his cheeks rhythmically, as the heroes in old movies do after applying aftershave. Inside, the dance music resumed after a considerable pause, and instead of circling in time to the music, he balanced on one leg and looked back over his shoulder and up at the sky, which appeared to him more open than ever before, while at the same time his dead child came to mind, a thought more painful than any other. How fruitful, how incomparably substantial and spatial the sky could appear when one looked up at just the right moment—still appeared—no object more spatial, no space more substantial. And from this moment on, all that was over, at least for the present. Not unlike a shoemaker who steps from the sunny street into his dim workshop, to spend the rest of the day there, or a miner who disappears down his mine, and not for one shift only, Don Juan stepped over the threshold, back into the hall; these are the images at any rate that came to him as he was telling the story.

Previously he had taken in not only the bride but also various others in the hall. He saw his servant, for instance, bantering with the ugliest woman present and laughing excitedly, as one might with a real beauty. He noticed especially that the young fellows kept going to an open window and spitting in the direction of the Caucasus, perhaps an ancient wedding custom. He saw the orthodox priest arriving from the neighboring village after a long hike over hills and through rocky gullies. His floor-length black soutane was spattered up to the knee with yellow clay and pollen from the broom blossoms.

Standing in the doorway, he raised the fingers of his right hand and moved them first vertically, then horizontally through the air, blessing all those present, while his deeply tanned face, not sweaty in the slightest, glowed, and a longish object, very thin, and light in color, with a pointed end, stuck out between his lips—a toothpick. He saw all the wedding guests, including the infirm and the children, stand up as best they could for a succession of toasts—at least those who were sitting down—all ears for the person or subject being toasted, and saw that for the duration of the toast it remained ah, so quiet in the hall.

Now there was nothing and no one but the unknown woman. Even before this moment the bridegroom at her side had hardly been present, or present at most as a silhouette, no, not even as a silhouette, as just a shoulder, a flash of white shirt, a moustache. Now he no longer mattered at all. He was completely interchangeable, not even a placeholder or a substitute—a meaningless X in the equation to be solved. It was an equation in which only two givens counted: he, Don Juan, and she, the bride over there. Which bride? No bride was sitting there anymore, only the woman. And this woman, like all the other women who in one way or another became his in the course of the week, indescribably beautiful.

He went on to tell me that as he remained standing in the doorway he saw her as close up and as large as through a telescope, and above all as exclusively so—as, for instance, one can focus one's binoculars on a single cherry, or train one's telescope on the moon, a full moon, which fills the entire lens, without a trace or a wisp of the surrounding night sky. And she had no need to look at him specifically; a second glance on her part, and the equation would promptly have lost all value; for she was worth something, was worth more than anything else in the world at that moment.

Don Juan was no seducer. He had never seduced a woman. He had certainly run into some who had accused him of doing so. But these women had either been lying or no longer knew what they were thinking, and had actually intended to express something altogether different. And conversely, Don Juan had never been seduced by a woman. Perhaps now and then he had let one of these would-be seductresses have her way, or whatever it was, only to make it clear to her in the twinkling of an eye that there was no seduction involved and that he, the man, was neither the seducee nor the opposite. He had a kind of power. But his power was of a different sort.

He, Don Juan, was in awe of this power. Perhaps he had been less self-conscious at one time. But for a long while he had been reluctant to use that power. He told me straight out, and in a tone that suggested neither pride nor vanity but was almost casual, that the women in question, at least in this story he was telling now, recognized their master in him, not at the first moment of meeting, but rather later, in the moment of coming to know him. The other men had been, and would be, what and who they happened to be, and those women regarded him, Don Juan, as their master, their sole master, for ever and ever (without "lord and"). And as such they laid claim to him almost ("almost") as a savior of sorts. Savior from what? Simply savior. To save them from what? Simply to save them. Or simply: to get them, the women, away from here, and here, and here.

Don Juan's power emanated from his eyes. It was superfluous to mention that this was not a technique he had developed. He never intended or planned any such thing. Nonetheless he was conscious in advance of the power or the significance conveyed the moment he laid eyes, or rather his eye, on the woman, not conscious in a masterly way but rather an almost anxious way.

The manner in which he avoided for as long as possible looking straight at the woman could easily be mistaken for shyness or cowardice, and it actually was, he told me, something like shyness, but cowardice not in the slightest! Once his eye came to rest on her, it meant: now there was no going back, for both of them, and it was a question of more than the present moment, or one night.

A philosopher once characterized Don Juan's desire as irresistible, even "victorious," perceived as it was by women as unconditional. But his story, as he told it to me, had nothing to do with victory and desire, at least not his, Don Juan's. On the contrary, the situation was that with his gaze—and not with his looks, which were rather inconspicuous—he unleashed the woman's desire. It was a gaze that took in more than her alone, and different things, a gaze that extended past her and let her be, and thus she knew it was directed at her, and appreciated her; an active gaze. Enough of playing around while walking down the street, while sitting and standing on railway platforms and at bus stops: at last things were turning serious, could turn serious, and she experienced that as a form of liberation.

From Don Juan's eye on her and additionally on the space around her, this woman came to a realization of how alone she had been until then, and recognized that this moment would promptly put an end to that. (During this entire week it was only lonely women of this sort whose paths crossed his.) Becoming aware of loneliness—the energy, pure and unconditional, of desire. And in the woman this expressed itself in the form of a demand, as unspoken as it was powerful, indeed "victorious," a demand that, if it came from a man, even such a solitary man, would certainly have no effect. Additionally, this demanding rendered the woman, even if she was a beauty to begin with, more beautiful still, beautiful to the point of impossible to-be-more-beautiful, whereas for a man such an expression . . .

Don Juan left open the ending to the episode with the bride from the Caucasian village, both in general and in detail. Nor did I want to hear any particulars, at least any definitive ones. Besides, the ending had been clear to me from his very first sentences. As was his habit, he described the actions primarily in the form of negations, especially when he became the active party, or he simply skipped over them, as something not worth mentioning. Thus it was enough for him to say that from the door to the hall he did not head for the young woman. And he had not thrown himself at her, or anything of the sort. Nor had they slipped out together to the next room or the outdoors. Nor had they exchanged a word, not "Come!" or "Now!" or "It's time!" And although they had been together without shyness or shame, as completely as two people can be together, openly and in broad daylight and surrounded by all the wedding guests, no one had had eyes for them, let alone noticed or seen anything; the alternative system of time that went into effect with their conjoining, however that came about, resulted in their no longer being visible, rather like those moving bodies that the human eye is not fast enough, but also not slow enough, to perceive as moving.

Don Juan did tell me, however, about various other things from this day that had stayed with him, in the forefront or back of his mind. He had one action of his own to report, though a rather minimal one: after he had finally circled toward the bride and with his gaze revealed himself dutifully to her from a distance, he had taken a few steps backward and thus created a magnetic field, to which the young woman yielded without hesitation, as if it were the obvious thing to do. Worth noting, perhaps, that when actions did occur in his narrative, Don Juan merely reported them quickly, whereas when it came to inner states and complications, he repeatedly gave himself plenty of time.

What made it easier for the two of them to approach each other was an incident that almost ended with a death. One of the guests got a fish bone stuck in his throat and was in danger of choking. The entire hall went into an uproar when the man jumped up from his seat, uttering piercing shrieks, which changed more and more into howling and whimpering, then into gasping, and finally into soundless flailing in all directions. By now the man had crumpled to the ground and was thrashing around on the floor, his face so dark red it was almost as black as an octopus. The people crowding about were shouting all kinds of advice as they bent over him. Except that the choking man could not hear anything at this point, and he convulsively spat out the chunks of bread that were stuffed into his mouth on the theory that they would push the bone down. In the end it was a look that then made him come to himself, and all this time he had been scanning the room pleadingly for such a look. Anyone could have supplied it; no special ability or training was necessary. For a moment he calmed down, and that was enough to allow others to help. They pounded him on the diaphragm, et cetera, and soon someone pulled the bone, or whatever it was, out of his throat, and so on.

It was not merely this person but the entire company gathered there in the hall that seemed to have been brought back to life. The others sat with the man, now that he was saved, and groaned, panted, and so forth, in sympathy. From one moment to the next, death had been omnipresent, and each of the guests had felt it break out in, not break into, his very own personal midst, and there was no one whose sense of life, no matter how tenuous, had not been enhanced by this outbreak of death, if not increased to the maximum, if not to the utmost. What joyful dancing now ensued, and among those thronging to the dance floor were some who had never danced before or had not danced in a long time, and the dancing was not wild or extravagant, at least in the beginning. And conversations sprang up among the few uninvited guests always expected at a Caucasian wedding and between relatives who had been on bad terms for ages, these conversations animated by the sudden increased flow of wine at the tables, on which, as was also customary in Georgia, several bottles were plunked down at once, even on the small tables. And here and there one saw a child, without benefit of wine, fervently kissing and hugging its father or mother, and it was clear that in the past these children had never embraced their parents, even fleetingly.

Don Juan and the young woman, now face-to-face as a result of the general tumult, had long since stopped breathing. Something else was breathing in their stead. When their time was then up, in a last blaze of gleaming splendor, which was both a privation and a deprivation, as minimal as it was crushing, and at the same time—as far as Don Juan was concerned—an acceptance of deprivation, they laughed, let go of each other, and turned away, their gestures and movements exact mirror images. He escorted the bride back to the bridegroom at the long table, walking a few steps ahead of her. What astonished him, experienced though he was from previous encounters, was that the gleaming and silent laughing persisted as they made their way there. The wooden floorboards gleamed. The apples from the previous fall, actually quite shriveled and dull, laughed and gleamed in a bowl. Even the spiders and daddy longlegs in the smoke-stained ornamental plaster molding had a sort of gleam. And outside, through the windows: what a sky! And he had not seen such clean snow in an eternity. Even the rushing of the wind had a gleam to it, accompanying the accordion inside the hall, the only instrument playing just then, so softly as to be almost inaudible, and not a folk song or a hit tune but a melody from *The Magic Flute*—an operatic aria interpreted with an accordion: again, Don Juan had not heard anything so tender in an eternity. They took each other by the hand, both hands, as if parting for a lifetime. He parted from her enthusiastically: the paradise of parting.

Yet as he turned toward the woman, he knew that she did not share his acceptance of absence and privation. Her eyes were black with anger, not anger toward him in particular but general anger, fundamental anger. What had just taken place between them could not be all there was. As far as she, the woman, was concerned, her time was not up, not in the slightest, would never be up. And thus he, Don Juan, discovered that he had to get away from her instantly—not that he wanted to flee, in fact he resisted the idea—but he had no choice. He returned her to her husband, who, by the way, gazed at him from afar as if he were a very dear friend, just as he, too, now that he finally noticed him, was filled with a sense of genuine friendship; and then it was: out of there!

That was what happened. Except that Don Juan's escape coincided with that of his servant. And the latter's was very conspicuous, in contrast to Don Juan's, offering all the features an escape can offer. His own escape was observed only by the deserted woman, by her eyes alone, and later, when he was already miles away, "out of shooting range," he thought, he could hear her grinding her teeth, spitting, and above all sighing. (Don Juan, who otherwise sighed all the time, had never sighed for a woman; there was never any question of that. It was simply not appropriate and would have demeaned the woman—and him.) The servant, however, fled with everyone watching, and he and his master, who was already waiting in the car, were pursued by any of the wedding guests who were mobile in the slightest. In classic style, not only did stones land in the dust behind the car (except that the dust did not form swirling clouds) but a veritable hot pursuit also occurred (except that it came to a sudden halt at the village limits, at the exact spot, as if this border, like the borders between American states, also marked the jurisdictional limits).

The old scratches on the servant's face had been joined by new ones, some of which continued to bleed for a long time. He drove without his elegant jacket, and his white shirt was ripped, the scratches extending far down his back. His lower lip was swollen, in its middle a single blood clot from a bite, the tooth mark clearly visible in the flesh. Shortly before they reached Tbilisi he regained his power of speech. After the scare with the guest writhing on the floor, struggling against death, he and the ugly woman had slipped away without another word, as if by previous agreement, and hurled themselves at one another. In truth it was more the woman who pulled Don Juan's traveling companion away and hurled herself at him in a kind of broom closet, et cetera. Yet he did not deny that he had had designs on the woman. He explained to Don Juan that to him she had not seemed ugly at all, from the very beginning, without even the additional influence of the festive atmosphere, wine, or excitement. Altogether he had always been attracted to those who were generally considered unappealing. The moment a pockmarked woman appeared on the scene, a kind of sympathy moved him. And at the same time he wanted to possess the woman, scars and all. He seemed downright embarrassed the moment a woman considered more or less unattractive in the conventional sense turned up—embarrassed with empathy and desire for conquest. He literally blushed every time this type of woman crossed his path, which Don Juan came in the course of the week to be able to predict— blushed and at first looked away, confused and almost crazed. And the fact that he pounced on such women was, according to the servant, not the result of a lack of taste, let alone a perversion. These women whom another man might see as slightly disfigured, and likewise those a bit past their prime, the wallflowers and ones who slunk along indoor or outdoor walls, were simply his type. With them he promptly undertook an adventure; no question of love's playing any part.

He had been caught with the "ugly one" in the broom or ironing closet, among the brooms or on the ironing board, caught by people who chanced to pass by and thought they were stopping a murder or involuntary manslaughter. It was because of the girl's local status that the entire Caucasian village then wanted to punish him for his action: she was considered feebleminded, and the feebleminded were considered untouchable, were strictly taboo; as a native, he should have known that. Yet he swore later to Don Juan that although he had been aware of the taboo, he had also known that his partner was not "abnormal." That had become clear to him earlier, as the hours passed. A person with eyes like that could only be normal, indeed on top of the situation. And what soft hands this supposedly retarded woman had.

By the evening of the following day, Don Juan and the other man were landing in Damascus. That was what I was told a week later. It goes without saying that I was not allowed to ask how they had got there. And I did not ask. It was enough that it seemed possible to me. Nor did I ask where Don Juan spent the night in Damascus, or where his servant slept. That was left to my imagination, as was the case with the next stages of the journey. But I did not need to picture settings, which would only have interfered with my listening, just as I did not need the Syrian weather report: it was clear that there, too, the May air was filled with swirling poplar-blossom fluff, and, as the story continued, I saw it rolling along the reddish yellow earth and floating past the likewise reddish yellow walls, while the material in its wake seemed increasingly weightless.

To Don Juan it was absolutely certain that on the very evening of his arrival in Damascus he would meet another woman. The coming period, of indefinite duration, would be a time of women, and one woman would lead to the next. As a result of becoming involved with the Caucasian bride—he did not say "with her"—he found himself in the sights of the special women who provided the subject of his story. That had nothing to do with a scent, as his servant, by now his confidant, contended in his tirade against all women (of which more later): "They can smell across seven hills when an available man is approaching." That he was received as someone they had ceased to expect stemmed from his entirely new readiness, or rather a readiness awakened for the first time, that affected those women quite unlike any passion for adventure, and was combined with obvious availability, as well as a sort of carefreeness or cheerfulness that promptly infected the woman of the day, making her almost saucy or, to be more precise, daring.

But what had the most immediate effect during the entire week was Don Juan's obvious temporal alignment with her, the other person, which at first sight caused her to experience herself not as the other, just as she no longer perceived him, the stranger, as the other. If there was anything the woman could trust, it was this alignment. That was something she could trust; as events took their course, the two of them would constantly feel or act in sync. She and he had a completely congruent sense of time. In Don Juan—if any name for him occurred to her, this was one it would never be—the woman encountered her contemporary. What she did not know, and also did not need to know, was that the availability as well as the carefreeness that Don Juan beamed in her direction derived largely from his persisting sorrow. His years of mourning were not past. His involvement with women made him aware more poignantly than ever of his misery over the loss of his nearest and dearest.

Don Juan told me less about his encounter with the woman in Damascus than about her predecessor in the foothills of the Caucasus, and less and less about the women who followed. Only this: it took place in the hall of the whirling dervishes near the Great Mosque, whose precise name did not come to him—I could have supplied it, but I was afraid to add my voice to his, the storyteller's, and besides, the name would have been too much for this episode; the Great Mosque of Damascus was good enough, just as in the following stories it was enough to say: by the fortress in the enclave of Ceuta in North Africa, on a dock by a fjord near Bergen in Norway, and so on.

During a concert that the dervishes accompanied with their dancing, Don Juan sat in the very last row. After a little while he no longer heard the drums, the lutes, the flutes (or shawms) as a concert, or as any kind of music. He heard nothing at all, was entirely a spectator, his eyes glued to the dancers in their wide, bell-shaped costumes, with towering cylindrical hats on their heads. The dance

consisted of bodies twirling around themselves, slowly for
the most part; when it speeded up, it paradoxically gave the
impression of slowing down, of majestic, imperious slow-
ness, including the garments, which whirled along with
their wearers, and their eyes, which gazed straight ahead,
motionless, as the dancers spread their arms, one hand
seemingly pointing to the ground, the other offered like
a bowl, to the heavens. Ecstasy? Impossible to imagine
anything calmer than these dervishes whirling themselves
around and for moments almost invisible, or anything more
inward focused. The majority of the dancers were older,
and for that reason the stillness that emanated from them
was even less astonishing. Yet toward the end of the
ceremony—for that is what it was, rather than a mere
performance—a very young dervish, hardly more than an
adolescent, took over the whirling from the old ones. He
spun lightly and at the same time with extraordinary seriousness, projecting an aura of distance, but by no means
emptiness, at eye level. And even at the end, when the spinning stopped, no smile, not even a flicker of one, at most
an openness in his face.

And now Don Juan saw himself singled out again in
that special way by a woman in the crowd. She was seated
in one of the front rows. And here it was she who turned
to look over her shoulder, for just one beat, it seemed, after the instruments fell silent and the dervishes' spinning
slowed to a halt. And again he did not describe the woman
to me—needless to say, she was "indescribably beautiful"—
but varied the account by mentioning that at first sight he

had taken her for a nun, because of her headscarf and her dark dress, closed up to the neck. But then he had noticed that most of the other women in the room, including those who were hardly more than children, were dressed in the same manner.

Much of what happened after that took the same course as the experience with the first woman, the one of the previous day in that other country, exactly the same in appearance and in tone (although a week later, he, Don Juan, could not recall a single sound, tone of voice, or utterance common to the two of them, whereas he retained vivid images of her alone, and even more of random objects in her surroundings). But it did not disturb him that most of what had transpired before was repeated, and repeated again, with the women on the subsequent days of the week, nor did it cause him to hesitate, let alone recoil—he had recoiled for a moment only the first time, when there was not yet any question of repetition. Instead the repetition developed its own dynamics, each time more powerfully, and he let himself be carried along as if it were entirely natural, a law he had to comply with, if not a commandment. That was how it had to be: he had to do or avoid the same things with this woman here as with the one from the previous day. The very repetition lent him courage.

Not that there were no variations. A variation played a part every time, though perhaps just a slight one, a tiny little one. The variation enabled the commandment to be fulfilled and at the same time became part of a game, became a commandment and a release, or, as his servant later expressed it, the variation provided the spice.

Day after day, the women themselves, eager to tell their stories and to be told, revealed their persons and lives to be largely repetitive. Up until then they had all lived in outrageous solitude; however, they did not become aware of it as an outrage, or indeed aware of it at all, until this moment. They were all natives of their respective countries, yet also conspicuously strangers. Otherwise they were all inconspicuous, as if without qualities, becoming beautiful only after their eyes were opened and they finally allowed themselves to be seen, and then they became indescribably beautiful. They all radiated something dark, even menacing, but it engendered fear only incidentally, at least in him, Don Juan. They were all of unspecific age, or seemed, whether young or less young, to transcend their ages. Wherever they were, each of them was on the lookout for the man who would be worthy of her, and they had enough presence of mind to leap into action, "in the twinkling of an eye." They all existed primarily as if they had always been on the verge of dying, going mad, picking up and leaving, striking someone dead. They all had the capacity to become dangerous. And even when there was nothing to celebrate, neither a wedding nor a dance, they all moved through the most mundane circumstances in a shimmer of festiveness, or even more a fragrance of festiveness—in retrospect he saw all of them, yes, all, in white. And not one of them spoke of people who were sick or dying, if they opened their mouths at all.

In a further instance of repetition, the outward conditions that brought the woman together with Don Juan represented each time a kind of threshold. The role of the fish bone in the Caucasian village was represented in Damascus by a sandstorm. In the enclave of Ceuta it was perhaps the war expected to break out the following day, and in the dunes of Holland, on the fifth day of the week's story, it was the spring flood bearing down from the North Sea. (Only in the case of the woman encountered on the day when Don Juan appeared in Port-Royal was there no need for an external threshold to provide the last impetus—the profound exhaustion both of them were experiencing was enough.)

The variations in the Damascus story Don Juan told me, and he limited himself from then on almost entirely to the variations in his encounters with the week's women, but described each one with a gleam in his eye: if in Georgia the floorboards had creaked under him and the woman there, here it was sand that crunched under them. He waited for the woman not in the midst of the crowd but quite far from there, way behind the mosque in a recently bulldozed area, a temporary no-man's-land. He was sure that she would turn up there, without his having to pace off the route beforehand by walking backward; it was a period when the women who constituted his tale's subject matter had selected precisely such areas as their own personal territory—the out-of-the-way places were their preserves—except that they had no intention of hunting or gathering; usually they had nothing more in mind than going for a stroll unaccompanied.

He had a long wait. Earlier in the day it had been bright and sunny, and now it was soon deep night. The sickle moon seemed a bit plumper than the hairline-thin one under which he had set out from the Caucasus. Obviously it would have been more than fine with Don Juan if the woman had changed her mind. What was in store for him was a test, and he had not the slightest idea what it would entail. He did not know what would be tested, and was not allowed to know, and the test would be more than just difficult; it would demand the utmost of him (even if that could also be handled with the greatest of ease). He had to wait for the woman to turn up. The rule was that he could not flee, not at this moment. Besides, she would track him down, here as elsewhere. At this hour there was no evading the woman.

She appeared as the moon was already veiled by the gathering sandstorm. No footsteps could be heard that might have announced her coming. She was simply standing there. Don Juan had stared into the darkness so long that any light, even the smallest, would have blinded him, and without any light source she moved sure-footedly in the dark, over the rubble of bricks, coming straight toward him as if it were completely natural. No breathing to be heard, either, although she had clearly been running. How silent those women could be, and how quickly they always appeared on the scene—in a flash they were there— and how mysterious they remained from beginning to end (no, no end), without any secretiveness or fuss over secrecy.

Strolling back and forth together in the shelter of what was left of a high wall, against which the gusts of sand hissed. A week later, Don Juan described the iron reinforcement material poking out of the wall and the unearthly music the powerful wind made in the tangle of wire, rods, and pipes above their heads. The assault of air and grains of sand on the iron was intermittent, at least for a while. For moments at a time it would gain in strength, then ebb a bit, then rise to a new crescendo, then weaken to a whistling, then to a mere fanning, whereupon it would set in again, more violently than ever, and so on, without ever dying away and ceasing altogether. The wind set up a constant reverberation in the iron fretwork sticking up into the storm, and whereas nothing but a howling, roaring, and pounding, thoroughly monotonous, would have been heard if the air currents had remained steady, instead a veritable melody took shape, something that was steady in an essentially different way. And it was a harmonic melody. True, its measures were all different in length, and between the highest and the lowest notes steps would have had to be added to the scales at the top and the bottom. But the transitions between almost inaudibly high and barely audible low notes, and the alternation between the shortest and longest measures, between loud and soft, did not occur abruptly or suddenly, by chance or at random, but rather always harmoniously, and in time blended in with the melody—in a number of languages the word for "time" was the same as for "measure"—the instrumental accompaniment being provided by the vibrating wire, the half-loosened iron rods drumming against each other, and especially by the system of pipes, open to the storm, which served as the leaders of the melody, so to speak, while the wire and rods created the rhythm. Don Juan hummed and sang the music to me, his voice scratchy at the beginning, then increasingly powerful, as he rose from his storytelling chair and with arms outstretched stalked up and down the Port-Royal garden, and I, who for so long have not been sure of anything, was sure that if he had performed this piece of music in public, it would have conquered the globe as hardly any other music could.

Eventually the Damascus sandstorm escalated to the point that it became monotonous after all. Except that after the previous melody, with its rising and falling notes, what one could hear from the iron latticework was not a monotonous howling and shrieking—although it was that, with an undertone of roaring— but the mighty finale. By then the two of them, the woman and the man, were lying behind the stretch of wall and listening. In the midst of all this Don Juan's heart was almost breaking from sorrow. But precisely this restored his strength. It allowed a person to transcend himself. The sorrow made one leave the personal behind. And its presence worked wonders. In the midst of the darkness and the storm, colors appeared. In the foliage of a half-stunted cherry tree in the rubble, the red of cherries suddenly became visible above the couple, without any obvious source of light. With blackness all around, a bluing of the sky. A powerful green-ing on the ground, which crunched under them. In this panic-stricken world, Don Juan felt at home. This world, if any, was his own. And there he came together with her, the woman. In the panic-stricken world they found each other.

Some language or other had the expression "in no time" for a certain kind of time or duration: "In no time he got from A to B." And Don Juan often used this ex-pression, and often, though in a somewhat different sense, for the story of the seven days of his womantime. In no time, for instance, as he lay with the woman beside him in that Damascus rubble, it was morning. In no time the sandstorm had given way to a softly whiffling prematuti-nal wind, "from Yemen," as the woman remarked out of the blue. Already roosters were crowing, city roosters as well as Syrian country roosters. Already turkeys were gob-bling all around—no, they had been gobbling all night long. Already peacocks were screeching—no, they, too, had screeched that way all through the night. In no time the voices of the muezzin were summoning people to morning prayers from the minarets, either live or on a crackling phonograph record or a buzzing tape. Instead of the sand, billows of exhaust fumes. Already contrails in the sun, already swallows, flashing upward in their swooping flight, already the glow of the poplar-fluff tufts as they drifted along high up in the air. And what was that squealing and bellowing, a persistent howling: here among the Arabs it could not be a hog on its way to the slaughterhouse; as the whimpering and sobbing now revealed, it could not be an animal at all—but neither could it be a person, at least not a big person, a grown person; or maybe it was an adult after all, abandoned by God and the world and crying as otherwise only a child would, and at least all the previous night, and continuing from now on without end.

The moment came when Don Juan and the woman returned, by mutual agreement, to ordinary time. (He noticed a bit later that in her case this was not entirely true, and as a result he had no choice but to get away as fast as possible.) They did not part immediately. He accompanied her home. She gave him her necklace, with Fatima's protecting hand. They breakfasted together, and her child, who was awake now, ate with them. At the table the child sat next to the stranger as if nothing were amiss. It took Don Juan's presence more than for granted. It beamed at him wordlessly, as if it had been expecting him for a long time. This stranger, whether he stayed or not, was a friend. Here a child took the place of the bridegroom in the Caucasus.

His servant was asleep in the next room at the inn. No response to Don Juan's knocking. The door was not locked, and he went in. Pitch black in the room, the window shutters closed tightly. Then a glow appeared, from a cigarette, and the next moment another, next to the first. No sounds except from the inhaling and exhaling of the smoke, in duplicate each time, and this continued for quite a while, until Don Juan tiptoed over to the window, as quietly as if he were the servant and the two in the bed his masters, drew the curtains apart, and even more quietly, if possible, pushed open the shutters. In the meantime the couple continued to draw on their cigarettes, without appearing to be blinded at all by the sudden daylight; it was like a nocturnal scene in a film. They acted at first as if the third person were not even there. For his part, he did not look at them directly, concentrating instead on the morning bustle out on the street, but from his quick glance at the servant and his woman he had gained an even more vivid and lasting impression, one that stayed with him long after his departure from Damascus. By the way, he told me later, if one refrained from looking directly at a thing and instead just brushed it with a glance, the image could burn itself onto one's retina in a way that no purposeful observation or contemplation could. Be that as it may: what he took in of his servant's new lover was only her striking ugliness or disfigurement, caused by acne, chickenpox, or leprosy scars, and along with that a shamelessly blissful smile, while her lover, whose bite marks or scratches from the previous days seemed to have healed overnight, puffed calmly on his cigarette while constantly plucking at the girl's hair, breasts, and, most insistently, her overly long and of course also crooked nose, with a facial expression in which fury and pleasure, tenderness and disgust, satiety and hunger, yearning and guilt, were inextricably blended (the latter had nothing to do with his master's appearing on the scene).

A week later, as Don Juan revisited that night and the next half day spent in Damascus, he offered the following meager details: a couple on the street below in front of the inn, the woman, already old, walking at a great distance behind the equally old man, a distance that remained the same, even though she seemed to quicken her pace and the man in front of her seemed to slow his. (A similar couple had also passed by in the Caucasian village, except that there the man was behind the woman, far behind, and she was walking slowly, while he was pumping his arms, his legs trotting along.) And a bird had sped from one grassy patch to the next, like a frog. And a child at a spring had tripped over the rocks around it and had tried for a long, long time to hold back tears. But then . . .

On the way to the enclave of Ceuta—this, too, in retrospect more a way than a journey—Don Juan was overcome by a monumental yawning. But it was not the kind of yawning caused by tiredness, like that of his servant, who was seated several rows behind him, as if he were a complete stranger, a fellow passenger who seemed to have no connection to his master during long stretches of their travels together. Don Juan's yawning was the sort that set in when one had barely skirted some danger. That was how one yawned after so-called last-minute rescues, hauled back to terra firma from the brink of a precipice, or in certain war comedies, actually not so funny, when the hero has just lit a cigarette in the middle of a battle and finds that all he has between his lips is the butt of a butt—that is how close the enemy bullet whizzed by his head. It was a hearty yawning. Now life, or his story, would not merely putter along somehow. Whisked to safety, Don Juan saw himself as more on the alert than ever. Confident that his safety was merely temporary and of short duration, he could also revel in it on the way through North Africa, while any other kinds of safety would have had the opposite effect.

Such reveling soon awakened happy anticipation of the woman, the stranger, who would be his lot at the next way station, and he in turn would be hers, and meanwhile he was looking forward, on this third day of his woman-week, not merely to the next one but also to the one after that. And at the same time he hauled his sorrow from one station to the next; his inconsolability. In this fashion a plan gradually took shape, without any effort on his part. He saw himself peacefully engaged in flight; his fleeing was peace itself; only in fleeing did he become so calm. Uneasiness seized hold of Don Juan again only as the next way station and the encounter with the woman approached. When it was almost upon him, he would have had no objection if a higher power—a fire, an earthquake, even the end of the world, for all he cared—had intervened. But during this period he soon realized that nothing could prevent the encounter. The state of war under way in Ceuta even made this encounter imperative, "as stated previously." From one day to the next no higher power intervened than that between him and the woman. Yet not a word about "love" from Don Juan. That would have merely attenuated what occurred.

As for the woman in Ceuta, Don Juan told me hardly more than that their first and definitive encounter took place far from any organized event. She did not follow him from a celebration or from any other busy scene to an isolated spot. She was there from the beginning, somewhere near the mined strip along the border, with its multiple rows of razor wire, which nonetheless did not prevent the peoples of the surrounding Moroccan and the more distant Mauritanian deserts from smuggling themselves by way of Ceuta, which was claimed by Spain, across the Mediterranean to the promised land of Europe. He was strolling behind the fortress there, and all of a sudden she was behind him. The woman followed him in that steppe of packed sand the way men supposedly follow women on the street, except that she never pretended that she merely happened to be going in the same direction or was headed for another destination altogether. He was her destination. Thus, whenever he looked back, she did not hide, either behind bushes or ruins—nor did she hide herself, not her eyes, not her shoulders, not her body; she pursued him with long strides, her arms akimbo, her head raised, her gaze fixed unwaveringly on him. Now and then she also tossed pebbles at him, actually empty snail shells. Now and then she seemed to have disappeared, and Don Juan liked that. He lay down on the bare earth, on his stomach, and fell asleep, and when he woke up he saw the woman walking around him in a circle, lit up by the spotlights along the border, which flashed incessantly, without a sound. And that was not all, he told me: her circles grew smaller and smaller, and finally the woman hiked up her dress and climbed right over the man lying there, and not only once but again and again, saying not a word, barefoot. And only then did Don Juan notice that the young woman was pregnant, and not in the early stages, either.

Later he spent much more time with an entirely different woman in Ceuta, a woman with whom not the slightest thing happened, as he immediately made clear. The following morning she came into the bar at the station from which the ferry departed for Algeciras. She was on the arm of his servant, and sat down next to Don Juan. She described herself as a vagrant and a conqueror, and he offered only an approximate account of what this conquering vagrant dished up for him.

She said she had once been the beauty queen of this Spanish enclave. It could not have been that long ago, yet apparently she was the only person around who remembered this fact. At first sight she seemed shapeless—Don Juan avoided using the expression "heavy," and certainly the term "fat" never crossed his lips. In her shapelessness she was nonetheless self-confident, even brassy, and thus it was not surprising that the servant had become involved with her—as was evident. While the woman was talking to his master about herself, he kept gazing at her from the side with that expression, familiar by now, of mingled revulsion and devotion. This time, however, his attitude revealed a third element, an air of abasement, and the revulsion was merely feigned, the devotion on the other hand slavish. It was also clear that she was not the one sitting next to him but that he, the man, was sitting next to her—at her side, merely tolerated, someone she was allowing to keep her, the woman, company for a while.

She had always—even as a child? yes, perhaps even as a child—wanted to get back at the opposite sex. There was no basis for this desire for revenge, not the slightest. She had not been raped by her father or her grandfather or an uncle, nor had she been cheated on or jilted by a lover. Very early in her life it had been enough if some boy looked at her in a certain way, not even on purpose, merely in passing—and from the beginning it was almost impossible not to notice her—and immediately she would react with the thought: That's it. Revenge. I'm going to get you. No sooner said than done, even when she was still a child. The boy would be lured into an ambush, then allowed liberties that made him completely vulnerable, and finally, as if nothing had happened (and in fact nothing had happened, nothing at all; it had all been for show, a dance of the seven veils), sent packing or made to "walk the plank," if possible in front of an audience, a male audience if possible, one member of which, thinking he was the new favorite, would become the next victim of her revenge campaign, and so on up to the present day: just as the schoolboys of long ago, robbed by her of all their illusions and banished from the world of childhood, would never find their way into a proper man's world, now she wanted to emasculate the grown men who became involved with her day after day and were promptly sent packing. Her revenge took the form of making them unsure, after their encounter with her, whether they were male or female. And she told Don Juan that it was not thirst for revenge but a passion for revenge. This passion manifested itself, in conjunction with her sexual passion, by the way, in the moment of her copulating with any man, and was promptly satisfied. She wanted him out of her. She did not even give the man the satisfaction of witnessing her rapture. As far as he was concerned, nothing had happened. A rude awakening from the most profound male dreams for him, to whom she had initially appeared as the paradise he had been seeking. "I was crazy. I am crazy. I will be crazy."

Yet this conqueror and avenger enjoyed the company of men more than that of women, incomparably more, infinitely more. And she said so in a voice that held not a trace of menace or scorn. Her tone was positively tender, and with that tone her face, as well as her whole body, emerged with a lovely suddenness from their shapelessness. Without any effort on her part, her lips took on contours; instead of bulges flaring nostrils appeared, and both eyes, suddenly and beautifully large, opened wide. Some of this, to be sure, was a deliberate effect; as she herself then demonstrated, achieving this transformation without the aid of cosmetics was part of the repertory she had early practiced in front of the mirror, thanks to which she had incidentally beaten all her rivals and become the beauty queen of Ceuta, going on to become Miss Spain. Yet practice played no part in what happened with her skin; as she conversed with the men (not "man," not "men" in general, but "*the* men"), despite the fact that her youth was long past, her skin became blooming, smooth, and glowing. And this was not the smooth face of one bent on

revenge, taut and unyielding. Apparently, as one could tell
from the few lines still visible on her forehead, it was a soft
smoothness, receptive though not needy, rosy, with lips
that now looked pale by contrast. What became taut and
ready for action was her body. Only men counted for her.
Women: the very word repelled her. Only men: now this
one, then that one, then another, and yet another—they
alone were worthy of consideration. And with each of them,
as was clear from the outset, without her formulating any
plan, she insisted on revenge. Every man, whoever he
might be, was to be won over, made to do her bidding,
then finished off.

In the bar of the Ceuta ferry station she now demonstrated this process to Don Juan on his servant, openly
setting her sights on yet another man. All she had to do
was cast her eyes over the place, and he came to her table,
as if on command. She whispered something in his ear.
He did not reply, just waited obediently in a special at-
attention posture, in fact slavishly, for what would come
next, for her further instructions. She then named a particular place, loudly enough for everyone in the room to
hear, and an approximate time in the evening. He al
ready had a ticket for the trip across the straits to Europe,
but would put that off, or—as one could immediately tell
by looking at him—cancel his plans altogether. She got
up to leave, without smiling, as indeed she had shown no
expression all the time she was talking, as if the person
listening were not even there. And in parting she did not
favor her lover from the previous night with so much as

a glance, even though he was there beside her, any more than she acknowledged his possible successor. Instead she turned to a couple snuggling in a corner of the room: "You two, mooning at each other like co-conspirators—you are so wrong about last night. On the contrary, both of you should be staring into the distance, bemused and bewildered, each of you bemused all alone."

Now she noticed Don Juan, and it was different from before: he was the one who made himself noticeable to her, as Don Juan; he did not say how (and I had long since stopped wanting to know). She recognized him and recoiled. Recoiled as from an apparition? As from *the* apparition. She had to get away from this person, her judge and executioner. It was true that she needed someone, needed this man or that intensely. But this particular man was the last she could have any use for. Never again should he set eyes on her. She could not grant him power over her, not for a second. No one could be allowed to prevent her from continuing to take revenge, not even this man. And thus the dignified departure of the former Miss Ceuta became an escape. In the end it was she who fled from Don Juan, and unlike his escapes, hers took place head over heels, without a moment's reflection, blindly, including movie-style collisions with the ferry passengers, knocking-over of metal drums, and the like.

It was also at that third stop during the week's travels that Don Juan opened his heart to his new servant. It happened as the two of them were sitting across from each other on the ferry benches. The other man was cowering there, white as a sheet, and it had nothing to do with the storm-tossed sea in the Strait of Gibraltar. People who had suffered embarrassment and humiliation like that were his people, Don Juan told me without explaining why, or, even in the form of this one man, they were his entourage, and in return he felt a powerful urge to provide a sort of escort for them, for him, even if it simply amounted to standing by them, or him, in silence. Thus, as they were about to sail from Ceuta, he had hauled his servant's luggage onto the boat—the man had almost three times as much as he did. He had found the best seat for him and taken it upon himself to show their tickets. And thus, too, he kept his servant company during the crossing and watched over him, staying by his side while at the same time looking away from him as the rocky enclave of Ceuta and the North African coastline receded into the distance, his back turned toward Europe as it drew near. And all of a sudden a flash emanated from the man that made Don Juan turn involuntarily and look at him. Tears had welled up in his servant's eyes, from one moment to the next, without a sound. And at the same time the man was grinding his teeth, as if to work up the appropriate rage to go with the tears. And the droplets of blood on his neck seemed to have just congealed. Needless to mention that the warming poplar seeds were migrating back and forth over this inlet, intersected on the perpendicular by masses of May hailstones, which, as they struck the waves around the ferry, caused innumerable sharp little fountains to shoot up.

Don Juan was still quivering with the memory of taking secret leave, in that same bar at the ferry station, of the Ceuta woman—his own. Secret did not mean secretive or surreptitious, however. She passed by outside on the dock in the company of an older man, and they nodded to each other, but openly, except that even the keenest observer would not have noticed this openness—such an observer least of all. These secret partings from his women, in a crowd, with people all around, at a distance, were the kind Don Juan liked, and in his eyes they were also the partings between a man and a woman most likely to go well; all other partings, he thought, were doomed to failure from the outset. And to go well meant that both their bodies took leave of each other secretly, from afar, their entire bodies. These two bodies had enjoyed each other, purely and simply, and now they felt pleasure again in the secret leave-taking, even more purely, if possible. At least he had a sense that a glow radiating at a distance from her body came over his own, whereupon he in turn, his gaze resting on her back—all he could see of her now—recognized that something entirely different was going on with the woman. She did not want a permanent parting—any more than the other women. He should not, must not, leave her forever. Her back, with the shadows of her naked shoulder blades playing over it, issued a threat: Too bad for you if you don't return! Her back demanded, it commanded. And in between her back also begged, quietly, pleadingly, as it disappeared into the distance. And Don Juan, engrossed in the scene, found himself looking forward all the more keenly to the next country and the next woman, felt all the hungrier for the next bodies that would come his way.

The old man walking with the pregnant beauty of Ceuta was her father, by the way, with whom Don Juan had sat harmoniously for hours the previous evening as they both gazed down at the sea, and in their sporadic dialogue each took the words out of the other's mouth, as if they had known each other a long time, and in the father's case known also meant trusted, indestructibly: Don Juan had nothing to fear from his back, and not because it looked so thin and emaciated.

The chief memory of Ceuta, as Don Juan described it a week later in Port-Royal, was the cinema, in which Don Juan sat alone, the sole member of the audience, and watched a film based on the *Odyssey*, in which Odysseus— at the end of the film, without a reunion with Penelope or his son—after seven years of sailing around was set down in his sleep by strangers on his own island of Ithaca, and when he woke up had no idea he was there, in the place he had longed for all those years. Then there was the lonely bar in that finisterre of Ceuta—no enclave in the world without this kind of land's-end bar—at the edge of the steep promontory where the African continent fell off, high above the channel, where the tavern keeper was a former Mr. Universe, still somewhat higher in rank than the local beauty queen, and for the benefit of Don Juan, his only guest, the man rippled his muscles one after the other under his now slack skin, imitating his victorious poses in the photos on the wall with a woeful smile, for a woman had just left him again, too. Then there was the tiny newsstand on the "Square of the Blessed Virgin of Africa," still open at midnight, the only place lit up in the entire darkened enclave, illuminated from deep within, a light that flickered only dimly through the newspapers and magazines hanging outside, but when one stuck one's head through the opening, with the vendor silently watchful behind the counter, the four walls were lit as if by flood-lights, no, not the walls, the unbroken shelves of books, not a patch of wall without a book's spine, and all the books for sale, now, during the blackout, with war threatening, a bookstore such as Don Juan had never come upon before, and how hard the book Don Juan was looking for—it was there, of course—had to be tugged at to pry it loose from the rest of the crammed-in inventory. And: the cancer patient on the ferry, whose hair had fallen out, had been at the wedding back in the Caucasian village. And likewise the village idiot, who strode with giant's steps down the empty alleys of the fortress, had already been there in Damascus, directing the crowd to the right or the left with command-ing gestures. And over there in North Africa he had al-ready encountered the motorcycle couple from whom he fled to me in Port-Royal.

It did not occur to Don Juan to do a count of the women during that week. Women and counting: the question did not arise for Don Juan, either then or ever before. He experienced the womantime instead as a time out. Not counting but spelling out. His womantime was a time in which there were no numbers. Nothing more to count, nothing that could be expressed in numbers. Having a time out meant that places and the distances between them, the stretches to be traveled, also did not count, did not embody any unit of measure. Being on the move was simultaneously a kind of constant arriving, and similarly, when he arrived, he thought of himself as still on the move. And he felt protected by this womantime, exempt from countingtime. As long as it was in effect, nothing could happen to him; even each of his escapes was part of his time out; every one was a new, quiet, positively calm escape, with eyes wide open. Womantime meant again and again: one had time. Was in time. In accord with time. Time kept striking a chord in one, even as one slept. And one felt time pulsing and warming one, down to the balls of one's feet and the tips of one's fingers. One felt not merely protected by this kind of time but borne along by it, and therefore instead of being counted, one was recounted by it. For the duration of such time one knew one was supported and transported in the process of being recounted.

There was not much for Don Juan to recount about the woman in Norway, other than that she waited for him behind a church, after the service, during which they had been more and more drawn to each other (nothing more natural and less frivolous, he told me, than for a man and a woman to have their eyes opened for each other, soul as well as body, by the celebration of the liturgy, far more naturally than by any other celebration).

Besides, according to local definitions, the woman was ill, disturbed, or insane. Except that Don Juan could not see any insanity in her and also did not want to believe it when she described herself as insane, that least of all. He simply wanted to be there for her, and then actually was—and how! At least that is how I pictured it, without his offering any details.

What Don Juan recalled from the day by the fjord, with the Norwegian woman: the wooden table outside; the soot on the spring snow (as just a little while earlier in the Caucasus); the light on the water, in the evening, which instead of disappearing became brighter and brighter for a while, as if for always; the moon almost the spitting image of the moon the previous day in Ceuta and the day before that in Damascus; the mirror-smooth red-and-yellow troughs left behind by the glacial tongue as it melted very recently; sitting there; being all eyes and ears; reading, reading, turning the pages, until the following day among the Dutch dunes, until the approach of the spring flood there. A fish leaped out of the fjord. An old woman passed by, her pocketbook dangling on long handles over her left arm, and how small this pocketbook was, and how empty it seemed. A man, even older, passed by, Chinese, his blue suit buttoned up to his chin, and gave everyone he met a wide berth, with a respectful manner that Don Juan found unforgettable. A child kept pushing buttons on a discarded boom box out on the bank of the fjord. A child, a second one or the same one, kept licking its plate, its face invisible behind the plate. A child, a third one or the same one, was missing, and all the people along the fjord set out to look for it, calling out over the desolate rocky landscape the name the mother had given them, until it was brought back, soaked to the skin but safe (only later did I learn who had found it, from Don Juan's servant, who had turned up again at last). Of course the teenager delivering pizza on his motor scooter was there as well; back in Ceuta he had failed to find his way to the customer, and here in Norway he kept speeding off in all sorts of wrong directions, only to slam on his brakes after a while in utter confusion. And on the head of the cancer patient, oh ho! a little fuzz of hair had grown back. And oh ho! the autistic person who had sat as if praying, legs crossed Indian-style, in the middle of the bus station in Damascus among the pools of oil, with his black caretaker beside him, was now lying on his stomach by the fjord, sleeping among the fish skeletons in the middle of the path that ran along the bank, his care taker sitting dark and silent next to him as in Damascus, arms crossed. And without Don Juan's having to mention it, I saw again those billows of poplar-seed fluff, silvery to mouse gray, blowing everywhere, up, down, and sideways, to north and south, as I already expected to see them at the next way stations, the one in the Netherlands and the nameless final one in Port-Royal. By the way, after the time with the Norwegian woman, Don Juan's servant disappeared for the time being, not without having prepared the most necessary things for his master's onward journey, and more than that: socks darned as meticulously as otherwise only a woman could do, and likewise his suit and shirt pressed, the buttons sewn on so tightly they could not be ripped off, all ready for any escape, his shoes gleaming up to the tongue, the smallest wrinkles polished, with bouncy new soles as if they belonged to Seven-League Boots. So Don Juan was fleeing again? He merely hinted to me that in the end he had had to run, lest he become the woman's murderer—a murderer on demand.

He had even less to tell about the woman in Holland as a person—which to my ears as a listener did not necessarily convey disappointment or satiety: on the contrary, Don Juan's storytelling grew more enthusiastic from day to day. His eyes, which almost constantly gazed past me into thin air, glowed. In the end he seemed astonished at the turns his story was taking, as one perhaps becomes astonished at something one has experienced because in the telling it sounds more and more made up, which, however, does not mean in the slightest that it is untrue—and it was only in such moments of amazement that the listener, to whom Don Juan otherwise merely showed the side of his face, found himself the recipient of a piercing look.

It was probably also part of this astonishment at what he had experienced, growing from weekday to weekday, that the sites of Don Juan's adventures became increasingly nameless (as the women had been from the beginning, as was only proper). In the case of Norway, the fjord still had a location, near the city of Bergen—or perhaps I merely supplied this detail while listening; as for Holland, no place name was mentioned at all. The only thing Don Juan told me about the woman there was that she had met him, the man on the run, out on the artificial dune, actually a covered and compacted landfill, she on the run as well, pursued by a pimp for whom she had been supposed to prostitute herself exactly a week earlier, but she was in no sense "that kind of girl." (In his narrative Don Juan was using the present tense more and more, and when he came to the last way station, he offered me almost nothing but cues.) The only other detail about the Dutch woman: she sits with him at a window overlooking a *gracht* or canal poplar seeds blowing, et cetera—while a May rain plops into the mirror-smooth yet dark water, and the woman, with tears in her eyes, all of a sudden says, "That's Holland for you."

Otherwise I saw, or sensed, Don Juan completely alone there for a day and a night. Only a dog, homeless, or perhaps not, keeps him company for a while, sometimes even running ahead and waiting for him, as if to show him the way. Dust flies up from the streetcar tracks. In a pine forest Don Juan pulls a thorn from the paw of the dog, which is still with him, and then on the promenade trims the dog's nails with a penknife, so the two of them will not make so much noise walking along on the pavement. During one of the day's many rain showers he sits under the roof of a snack bar by a bicycle path and reads the book he acquired at that very different stand in North Africa, the book's pages, as well as his hands and feet, constantly sprinkled with raindrops, sits there in the changing light and reads and reads, the dog next to him in the grass, or perhaps not. But wherever he walks, stands, and sits, Don

Juan is startled, and he turns his head suddenly and jumps up and runs off whenever he hears a child calling or even shouting, and on this day he hears children's shouts everywhere, or imagines them when a gull mews or the streetcars screech as they round the bend. Toward evening, in the strip on the horizon over the North Sea there appears the ship of the Argonauts, empty, without Jason, without the Golden Fleece, and Medea leaves the beach and goes into the house to kill their children. As darkness falls, all of Holland takes on the appearance of a land of neon and candles, and on all sides music is turned up, and each time Don Juan tries to get away from the music, away from the music, from this kind as much as from that. Instead he sniffs at the flower shops, long since shuttered— smells everything but tulips—sniffs at the book, sniffs his own fingertips, womantime, fingertiptime. And finally late night, peace and quiet at last, the quiet of the ocean, and at last, after all the preceding nights, the full moon, to which the solitary walker on the one hand constantly looks up, while on the other hand gazing into the conveniently curtainless houses, to catch the television news, and so on. Don Juan certainly had a song to sing about that day, and in fact he spoke of it in a singsong, or I am the one imagining that now. And the abrupt cessation of the singsong, and then another flight.

And then the last country, completely nameless, with the last woman. It was not that Don Juan withheld the country's name from me; he did not know it himself, from the very beginning, had no desire to know it. He did not even know how he got there, had no image of the trip (yet he must have used some form of transportation). Opening his eyes, after overwhelming tiredness: he was there. And the woman was there, on top of him, under him, facing him. Again he had no idea how the two of them had come together, and there was nothing to know there, either. No words to describe anything in their surroundings, and yet all around was the very opposite of a jumble. Not merely the fact that the place and everything there seemed so unknown and unnameable, since one simply did not care: it signified the height of amazement, without any form of magic it was magical.

Seven days later, when Don Juan told me about the day of namelessness, actually stuttering and stammering in confusion, he did not even know, in regard to himself and the woman, who remained a stranger to the end, which of them had said what, which of them had done what. (And they had stayed together for almost the whole day and for the whole night, a deviation from the week's pattern.) Don Juan no longer knew: Had he read aloud to her, or she to him? Had she eaten the fish or had he? Had he warmed her up when she felt cold, or wasn't it rather she who warmed him? Had she won the chess game or had he? Who caught up with the other when we went swimming—was that you or me? Who hid from whom for a while: you or me? Who talked and talked: she or he? Who listened the entire time: you? me? me? you? And that one did not know: as it should be. Let us be glad.

What did remain certain was that in that no-name way station the still childish pizza-delivery boy on his motor scooter, a Global, was trying to find his way, in vain (he had also run out of gas); that the autistic man and his caretaker, the former bawling up at the sky, the latter holding him by the arm, were continuing their two-person procession; that the motorcycle couple set out for their love hollow (except that there the woman still had black hair, not blond); that the old man from Damascus and Bergen was again stuck in the gutter, breathing hard and unable to lift a foot, either the right one now or the left, to place it on the sidewalk . . . Don Juan did not even have to mention these cues by now. As time went by, I saw these scenes all the more clearly when he refrained from describing them.

Don Juan and the women: this story, told by him himself, was thus at an end. He and I had spent seven days out in the garden this way, and in the meantime Pentecost was just around the corner. The hazel branch that had heralded his arrival was still stuck in the ground, hidden by the grass, which had shot up during the week like wheat. Even when it rained one time, we stayed outdoors, under the chestnut tree and then under the lime tree, whose foliage was so dense that hardly a drop got through, the roof of leaves over our heads almost solid, with only specks of sky visible, like flashes of daytime stars here and there against the dark green lime firmament. During the final phase Don Juan got up from his seat more and more often and paced as he talked, going backward. When the sun shone and the May wind wafted through the trees, the alternation between almost white light, quivering, and dark shadows became so powerful that for moments Don Juan disappeared from sight.

When his tale of the weeklong adventures was over, he stayed on at my inn at Port-Royal-in-the-Fields. Because he was waiting for his servant, or for whatever reason: I did not ask. I was happy that Don Juan did not set out again immediately. I had even come to appreciate his presence. The ideal of neighborliness, which has been with me all my life, and at which I thought I had failed once and for all in my hermit's solitude in Port-Royal, was reborn with this stranger, this fugitive, close by. I could picture Don Juan as my neighbor, if not right on the other side of the inn's wall then certainly at a distance of a few miles, perhaps over on the slope of Saint-Lambert. Altogether, thanks to his stay, I stopped, at least for the time being, thinking of myself as a failure. Even the way he ate the dishes I cooked for him: it had been an eternity since I had seen anyone eat so reverentially; his chewing was like a prearticulation of what he later put into words. It was not only a neighborhood that I could thus imagine having once more, but also my inn—serving guests again, which as far back as my childhood had been my favorite game.

During our seven days Don Juan had stopped letting me serve him all the time; he lent a hand himself. I had always found it difficult to accept help, especially given my small kitchen, but the limited space even made for a certain pleasure when he was there. It was already a pleasure, mixed with envy on my part, to watch him at work. Not merely that Don Juan was almost dizzyingly dexterous; he managed to carry out completely contradictory actions with both hands or arms, the sort of thing that had always brought me to the brink of despair in my profession, and not only there. I am capable of hope-lessly messing up even the simplest operation—for instance, pulling something with my right hand while pushing something else with my left. For him, however, it was no problem to slice an onion with one hand while rolling out dough with the other, let us say. The same was true of rolling with one hand and dotting with the other, piercing and smoothing, hollowing out and filling, throwing and catching, emptying and filling, as if in a single, coherent movement. While his right hand was roughing something up, his left was smoothing it. While he plucked at something, he pounded. While he spooned something out, he was crushing something else. While he was sawing, he was driving screws. While he was tugging, he was stroking. While he was turning a page, he was hammering a nail. And with all these actions, left-handed and right-handed, Don Juan proceeded with perfect control, slowly, and apparently slowing down even more, as if he were mindful, of a person or a thing, while carrying out any operation. That is how I saw him at work.

Now the seven days in the garden were past, and gradually that impression dwindled. Don Juan seemed increasingly clumsy to me. He reached for the wrong object, dropped things, acquired two left hands. Besides, he kept looking at the clock, and mentioned the date of even the most trivial happenings. The book containing Pascal's letters to the provincial resident of Port-Royal, from which he had read aloud in the evenings and which had made us laugh as only Molière's comedies could do otherwise, remained unopened. I saw Don Juan give in to a compulsion to count. He counted, at first only moving his lips, then out loud, his footsteps, the buttons on his shirt, counted the cars in the Rhodon valley, counted when a flock of swallows swooped over the garden, even tried to count each of the poplar-seed clouds. Yet it was something other than boredom. Time had not become boring to Don Juan. It was not that there were too few events or significant moments; on the contrary, there were too many, far too many. Every moment—every thing   was significant, and time had become fragmented into a second, a third thing or person. Instead of the coherence that a sense of time created, nothing but details, no, isolated elements. Instead of slow and careful he now seemed awkward and ponderous, or clumsy, as I said, or he rushed and was equally clumsy. Don Juan was having trouble with time. And every other minute he asked me what time it was.

To let him leave would not have changed anything. And I did not want to let him go so soon. Besides, he himself did not want to leave Port-Royal yet. So on the day before Pentecost I took Don Juan along to the village churchyard of Saint-Lambert. Seeing only my garden from morning till night: perhaps that contributed to his time-sickness. But going out into the apparent freedom of nature and stretching his legs did no good. For Don Juan the landscape remained an interior in motion, no different from my house with its walled garden. To look at him, one would have thought he was imprisoned under a thick glass dome. At every step he bumped into a tree,

stumbled off the path into the wetlands along the Rhodon, swiped at a mosquito, which was actually a wild dove
flapping along high overhead. The time crunch he had
blundered into also made him lose his sense of distance
and space. When we finally came in sight of the wonder-
fully broad plateau of the Île-de-France—which I involuntarily thought of as "mine"—I exclaimed, "Look at
that sky!" whereupon Don Juan merely asked, "What sky?"
When one of his shoes lost its sole as we were going uphill, and I commented that that was a sign of good luck,
he answered, "Anything but good luck, please!" which
meant something different from his repeated exclama-
tion during our days in the garden, "Boldness, not love!"
He hobbled behind me like a clubfoot, hanging his head,
whereas the previous week he had always marched in
front, directing me toward a distant goal with his eyes
alone. The animals especially became his enemies. Whereas
in the course of the week the cat from Saint-Lambert had
lingered longer and longer on her rounds and finally had
even brought company with her, now, as we walked along,
Don Juan felt under attack from the butterflies and the
newborn dragonflies. The tiny jumping beetles were now
jumping at him. The most innocuous spiders were hurl-
ing poisonous threads in his face. The first early crickets
sounded to him like annoying clocks being wound, the
first grasshoppers swishing through the grass like even
more aggravating ticking. And although we had hardly
any encounters, I heard behind me his constant, furi-
ous counting—counting of animals, of misfortunes, of
mistakes.

What struck me on the way to Saint-Lambert, however, was how much had changed there since the seven days spent with Don Juan's story. As I had always hoped, foreigners had finally moved into the village. At least the one store there, which had seemed closed for good, was open now as if for its first day—its grand opening—and in the doorway stood an Indian in a turban, while a young Chinese couple came around the corner, holding the map of hiking trails in the Port-Royal area. Altogether, after my week with Don Juan, all these distant neighbors (yes, neighbors) seemed rejuvenated. The old-timers, the money-hoarders as well as the stingy senior hiking groups, had disappeared from the region. I sensed business booming. And something had changed even in the few remaining longtime residents, as I noted when we passed through: for the first time in all these years I was seeing one or the other outside the usual terrain between their houses and the expressway. They were in the riparian forest, picking the wild cherries, which had just ripened, along the edges of the woods, picking the first wild strawberries. The few times when I had encountered such a gatherer previously, he had been ashamed of what he was doing (or had not been from around there); but now all these people, foreigners as well as locals, were out gathering perfectly naturally, if not self-confidently, and I was able to imagine that all of them, the new ones in the village as well as the old ones out here, would soon become good customers of mine.

For Don Juan, however, even these few people were far too many. They deprived him of what little space he still had, and threatened to push him out altogether. He counted the scattered figures in the seemingly vast Île-de-France as if they were members of an enormous hostile army. On the one hand he became strangely polite; he, who during the previous week had always waited until others greeted him, now was always the first one to utter a greeting, but so awkwardly, and at such a distance, that his greeting was not even registered at first, or if it was, then not as a greeting. On the other hand he seemed almost abrasive. He did not merely bump into the Asian couple, who were walking along holding hands. He rammed the two of them apart, forcing his way between them, head lowered, and it was not mere clumsiness, for at the same time he was uttering curses: What a disgrace that lovers from the Middle Kingdom were now holding hands in public, and so forth. But Don Juan's time problem, his suddenly erupting "tactlessness," manifested itself most clearly, it seemed to me, in his new desire for music, of whatever sort. Whereas previously during our time together he had scrupulously avoided music more than anything else, now he seemed positively addicted to melodies, rhythms, notes. He asked me in all seriousness, while we were still in the cemetery, whether I didn't have a Walkman with me.

Even there he at first continued his tirade of counting and cursing. He counted all the graves and cursed the caretaker, from whose lodge a clothesline was strung across the graveyard, as so often in France, with not only tablecloths but also sheets hanging out to dry, "and red checked ones, too!" I would have been tempted to laugh, had he not been quivering. Don Juan was trembling. He was shaking, and not in any rhythm. The only moment when it stopped was when he contemplated the empty row in back, between the Saint-Lambert graves, dedicated to the memory of the nuns of Port-Royal, who had once been branded as heretics and driven from their cloister because they had deemed divine mercy something that could not be taken for granted and was not readily available to everyone. (In his history, Jean Racine, who attended their school when he was very young, honored those women by calling the region of Port-Royal "un désert," which in his day meant something more than merely "a desert.") At that moment Don Juan described the trench or hollow that allegedly holds the remains of the nuns as "sublime," whereas normally this word describes something elevated, something rising above its surroundings.

Another moment for a time out came as we sat on a backless bench behind the churchyard, by what had once been a playground, an artificial mound with steps up its side, hardly any wooden treads left, only the eroded clay, a little pyramid that had taken on a conical shape and was now overgrown with brush. At our feet was sand with little depressions where sparrows usually bathed, each of the depressions renewed annually in the same spot by the current crop of birds, and all the birdbath marks in the sand forming a sort of constellation, Ursa Major. The Great Bear and sparrows: that went well together. Don Juan counting the hollows; this time without the counting compulsion.

And along with it the sighing with which I was by now so familiar. Who was it who said that sorrow had to be something that weighed one down? Then it was Don Juan who brought up the sky, when he finally raised his head and exclaimed, "Now that's a sky for you!" Finally children showed up after all, two of them, to play. They played a couple madly in love, gasping and groaning, and in the end both their tongues were hanging out.

When we got back, in front of the inn at Port-Royal the servant's car was parked at last. It was just as I had pictured it from Don Juan's story: an old Russian model. The servant himself, however, was at first different from the way I had imagined him, as was usually the case with those I had come to know only from hearsay. Involuntarily I looked for the scratches and bites on his face. But it looked perfectly fine. Only his moustache seemed to be singed in one spot, and what I at first took for a very un-servantlike ruff turned out to be one of those cervical collars that people wear after suffering whiplash. As we approached, the servant stayed in the car, sitting bolt upright and staring straight ahead. Although we stopped in front of and next to him, it was as if he did not notice Don Juan and me. He was in the middle of a monologue that could have begun infinitely long ago, his voice almost inaudible, like that of a sleepwalker, and this was all I could make out:

". . . woman and death. Whenever I went to you, I was prepared to meet my death. In fact you came hurtling toward me as if to kill me, but then you fell into my arms.

At least in the beginning. The danger of suffocation came afterward. The imprint of your cheek on the window, which I haven't wiped off to this day. Even from the doorway you cast a shadow that darkened the entire house for me. Oh, how I took pleasure in your darkness. You had hardly arrived when I no longer knew my way around my own room, and not merely because you immediately filled it up and moved everything around, and then moved it around again. Only back in the deserts, in the Arabian and Chilean deserts, were we man and woman. Ah, how your sparse hair, streaked with gray, moved me. Breathing in your smell made me sing, and when I sing that really means something. And once you were lying there, you lay there, and lay, ha! only a woman can lie that way, and lie, and lie, and between you and me lay your child and pressed its damp diaper into my face all night long. How unmistakably you were where you belonged, a woman alone, without a man, in charge, as only a woman can be. 'Come!' you said to me, and thought, 'Die!' Why didn't I simply let you pass—which you prefer to do anyway, and which makes you most exciting, in passing? Back to the deserts with you. In this country you now live in a constant rush, and still think the way you go storming through cities and suburbs from morning till night is beautiful. What a mistress of little signs and allusions you used to be—and what do I need more than little signs—and now you have no time for even the smallest of signs. No more messages on the windshield, under the doormat, in my jacket pocket; no more notes in my shoes, to be felt only after I have left you and am walking down the street, no more allusions—the more mysterious, the more durable. 'You are very much desired,' I told you. And you: 'By whom?' And I: 'By me.' What free hands you had in the desert, and how weighed down you are of late, wherever you go, how you drag yourself along, so unlike the way you were during that time in Africa and as a Bedouin. Where are you, women? Ah, instead only deals being offered, at bargain prices. Ah, but how seeing your buttocks passing still fills me with hope, with joie de vivre. Why in the world did I set out every day to find you? To get rid of my male crudeness, to penetrate your secret. And now? Trapped in even more dismal crudeness. I will stroke, shake, rattle, and beat the child out of you, you fiend of a woman. Next to us the leech that grew fatter and fatter while we made love. As you were grabbing my predecessor between the legs, you cast your first glance at me over your shoulder. You want to see me dead, woman, so you can mourn me. My neck injury was no accident; my head jerked back by itself, with the force of a heavy stone. I go looking for you, and when you refuse to show yourself, at least I will have gone looking. You wonderful unavoidability. Go ahead and croak. And tomorrow is Pentecost." Here the servant suddenly turned to his master, Don Juan, and his tone changed: "Hey, why don't you interrupt me? I can speak clearly only when I'm interrupted. And you, you keep silent on purpose, to let me go on flailing around." And getting out of the car: "Ah, I can express things only by talking in circles and taking detours. Ah, if only I were a poet. Ah, isn't it powerful that I'm here, and that at the same moment I have a hundred different things in my head. Ah, not until she slipped out of her clothes did I notice that she had nothing on. And even though she undressed in front of me, there were no clothes falling to the ground. That made her all the more naked. Who can understand that?"

As the three of us were having supper together, my inn was suddenly surrounded by women. Thinking back a week later to that bright evening in early May, I can hear piercing war cries, which in actuality were never uttered. Likewise I see the six or seven women all dressed in white. Instantaneously—the old term "straightaway" would describe their arrival better—they were there outside the walls, coming from all directions, one landing as if with a parachute, the other riding up on a horse, the third seeming to have just dismounted from an elephant, and so on. The women gazed at me grimly when I was the first to show myself through one of the slits in the garden wall, and they made me think of that forest of pointed spears I had once seen passing, over the top of the Port-Royal walls—which, however, when I saw it again outside the gate, merely belonged to a group of young athletes on the way to the field where they practiced the javelin-toss. "Fort Royal" (instead of "Port-Royal") came to my mind at the sight of those beautiful women laying siege to us. And they were beautiful, I can tell you that. Don Juan had not been exaggerating when he used the expression "indescribably beautiful." Even I, who saw myself as long since out of the running when it came to women, promptly thought, in spite of all the grim faces, "Count me in again." With these women something could still happen—God knows what. And once more I thought the sky was playing a role that day: ah, all those women there beneath the sky. Even if all the signs suggested that their intentions were anything but good, I was captivated by them. When those women out there act in unison, things will be popping! Except that these women did not act in unison. They did not so much as notice one another. The others did not exist. Even if one of them had run the woman next to her over, they would not have noticed each other. Each of the women was laying siege to Port-Royal by and for herself. Each of the "indescribable beauties" clearly existed without the others.

Yet one thing of beauty or another did become describable for me, as was fitting in the presence of those women. In the hill forests around Port-Royal the edible chestnuts had just come into bloom, and the cream-colored strings of blossoms hung down among the dark oaks like crowns of foam atop waves, seething on all sides in the area surrounding the ruins, and from the silent surf rose, at the very top, back on the Île-de-France plateau, the pale red roof of the former cloister stables of Port-Royal, a roof with a tile landscape more beautiful and strange and yet more dreamily familiar, as part of a barely discovered planet, than anything I had seen before, and the swallows swooping above it into the last sunlight moved twice as fast, as if propelled by the light. Of course down in the Rhodon valley the poplar seeds were drifting by again, the last batch, so to speak, whirled straight up in the air from the furrows in the paths, meadows, and plowed fields, interlocking more and more to form airy balls and scarves, and eventually piling up like fleeces at the women's feet, stuck together, while individual seeds continued to swirl around them, tickling their ears and noses, which the women acknowledged with slight grimaces and also with sneezes, without any softening of their grim expressions. A slapping sound in the air of that May evening as if from the soles of running children, yet none appeared. In the meantime the weapons in the hands of the women laying siege to us had come to resemble gifts.

"It's time!" I heard Don Juan saying behind me. A triple sighing became audible; the servant sighed, too, and yes, I did then as well. When Don Juan showed his face instead of mine in the loophole, the grim expression in the eyes of the six or seven women darkened even more, except that now it was grim in a different way. The faces they made now: wasn't the tickling of the poplar fluff to blame? A week later, I no longer see them as a number. If the question were asked: numbers or letters? I would reply: letters. What adds to that impression is that Don Juan is moving his lips as if he were spelling something out. Although it "was time," he gave himself time. The animals in my garden—the strange cat, the stray dog, the goat— also seemed to want to prevent him from stepping through the gate into the great outdoors. One animal dashed between his legs in a panic, another blocked his way, the third even stuck out a leg, obviously meaning to trip him.

Even the servant, who was preparing him for his big scene like a page, constantly making the wrong move as he was distracted by the perhaps merely imagined louder and louder whistles from outside the walls, contributed to the confusion. Don Juan, however, consistent with the earlier story, showed himself perfectly at home amid the panic. He looked around, completely calm, with the calm of a savage.

During his seven days in my garden, a whole series of Don Juans had shown up, in the evening programming on television, in the opera, in the theater, and likewise in what is called reality, in flesh and blood. Yet from what my Don Juan told me about himself I learned the following: those were all false Don Juans—including Molière's, including Mozart's.

I can attest: Don Juan is different. I saw him as someone who was faithful—the quintessence of faithfulness. And he was more than merely kind to me—he was considerate. And if I have ever encountered a fatherly person, it was he: one listened to him and believed him. Yet during those seven days he remained nicely distant from me, which suited me and also pleased me, a person whose dreams for a long time have focused only on others and on the stories of others, in which I do not occur. During our time together he hardly ever looked at me, only past me or through me, particularly while he was telling his story. Once he did look at me, however—and how!—when something like a talisman fell out of his hand and almost broke. A name escaped his lips—not that of a woman—and I caught the talisman, or whatever it was, in the nick of time.

Just before he opened the garden gate, however, I saw him laugh and wave to those outside. Out there I saw someone also laugh and wave, a man who had come out of the riparian forest and joined the women. And over his shoulder Don Juan told me that this was the brother of one of the women, the Norwegian or the Dutch woman or a third one, and unlike the woman, the brother had established friendly relations with him as he was leaving the country; what else was possible? The rest of the story cannot be told, either by Don Juan or by me, or by anyone else. Don Juan's story can have no end, and that, on my word, is the definitive and true story of Don Juan.